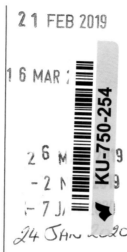

Annie O'Neil spent most of her childhood with her leg draped over the family rocking chair and a book in her hand. Novels, baking, and writing too much teenage angst poetry ate up most of her youth. Now Annie splits her time between corralling her husband into helping her with their cows, baking, reading, barrel racing (not really!) and spending some very happy hours at her computer, writing.

TEMPTED BY HER SINGLE DAD BOSS

ANNIE O'NEIL

MILLS & BOON

Published in Great Britain 2018
by Mills & Boon, an imprint of HarperCollins*Publishers*
1 London Bridge Street, London, SE1 9GF

ISBN: 978-0-263-07912-8

MIX
Paper from
responsible sources
FSC™ C007454

This one goes with a big fat happy heart to Susan, who corralled us together, Christine, who kept us sane, and Karin whose spirit kept the flame well and truly burning. You're all amazing. I'm so delighted to have 'discovered' Maple Island with you all. Perhaps we'll meet there again one day? Big love x Annie

CHAPTER ONE

"Ow!" MAGGIE HADN'T meant to yelp. Keeping her cool for her young patients was paramount.

Had the ferry surfed a huge wave or hit something? *Just make sure the children are unhurt.*

"Everyone okay?"

She heard a pair of yesses as she peeled her hands off the ambulance floor. "Looks like the ocean's a bit rough outside of Boston Harbor, kiddos. Maybe the ferry captain's seen Moby Dick!"

Without looking, Maggie knew her knees would be bloodied and a bump would be growing on her head. How she'd managed to fly past the ambulance's two vacuum mattresses and conk her head on the gurney wheels was beyond her. She quickly pushed herself back up to a sitting position and checked her patients. They were the priority here, not her.

The ten-year-old twins seemed fine, if a bit wide-eyed at the sudden movement. The ferry journey to the Maple Island Clinic hadn't been billed as a funfair ride. Nor was it meant to be. The weather had checked out fine, which was precisely why they'd opted for crossing on New Year's Day before the predicted snow moved in.

She looked down at her knees and saw a bit of blood seeping through the dark fabric as her right hand gingerly checked for...yup...a grade A head bump.

What a way to make a first impression at her new job.

She winced at the misplaced vanity as she tried to pull her wild tangle of red curls back into submission. This wasn't a beauty contest. Not landing on the kids had been the goal, particularly since their spinal injuries had been from collapsing scaffolding. The last thing they needed was her falling on them right after they'd been released from critical care.

She shoved away the rush of fear that had come with the sudden movement and reminded herself of her priorities.

Arriving at Maple Island with the children safe and sound was the goal. She was good at goals that involved patients. It was only the personal stuff that needed work.

"Billy, you all right up there?" She received a grunt from the paramedic who'd driven them onto the ferry. Better than a moan, she supposed. Or nothing.

"Looks like I should've stayed put and kept my seat-belt on, shouldn't I?" Talking endlessly wasn't necessarily going to calm them down but—

The piercing screech of the ferry's alarm came so short and sharp Maggie almost gave her roller-coaster scream. Not the best "responsible adult" response. She was meant to be soothing the patients, not freaking them out. As her last boss had constantly reminded her, not everyone was a finely wired adrenaline junkie.

Not everyone had to give themselves a reason to live at the age of thirteen, though.

Before she could get her seatbelt on, another lurch flat-tened her to the floor again. *Oof.*

"We've got a bit more than we bargained for in terms of adventure, haven't we, kids?" They both responded with something indecipherable beneath the screech of the siren.

Clonk.

A small tub of supplies found a perch on her head.

Mercifully the siren stopped.

Maybe it had been a pod of whales.

"Sorry, Maggie. Was on the phone with Vick. Everyone all right back there?" Billy stuck his head into the back as he untangled himself from the coiled radio cables. "Vick just doused herself in hot coffee up on the passenger deck."

"Ouch." Maggie winced. Painful way to get through a New Year's Day hangover. "Did she burn herself?"

"Nah. But she's going to check if anyone up there needs help. The weather's closed in. Total blinder. I'd better ring the clinic and let them know this isn't going to be a straight-forward journey." He held up the tangle of wires as proof the radio was out of commission. "Do you have the clinic's emergency number?"

Maggie glared at him then flicked her brown eyes toward the children. "Ixnay on the ary-scay alk-tay, my friend."

He looked at her blankly, then huffed. "I don't do pig Latin." He made a *gimme, gimme* gesture with his hand. "Number for the clinic, please, Mags."

Maggie recited it from memory, reminding herself that Billy had valiantly maneuvered the ambulance onto the ferry's small car deck when Vicky, the original driver, had announced an urgent need for coffee. They could've parked diagonally if they'd wanted to. Not one other car had followed behind them onto the dinky car deck. Had every other person in Boston read a different weather report from the one she'd had or were they all just hungover, like Vicky?

She'd checked the weather about a hundred times. It was meant to be calm today, snow tomorrow.

The clinic would go ballistic if anything happened to these two. And she wouldn't blame them. They'd been through enough. The terror of their house's scaffolding collapsing on them. Spinal surgery. Critical Care. Parents having to wage war with the insurance company and carry on working so they didn't lose what little money they did have. It had been a horrific holiday season for all of them.

The one silver lining had been the clinic taking them gratis. She wasn't going to let anything stand in the way of them getting the rehab they deserved. Not the weather. Not a cranky paramedic. Not on her watch.

"Actually…" she pulled out her own phone "…I'd better do it."

"Why?" Billy's arm shot out and only just missed her face as they both sought to stabilize themselves from another lurch.

"Because Boston Harbor's put me down as the contact and I'm the one signing the children over. My job. My responsibility."

"You're their physio. I'm in charge of the ambo, which makes me king of everyone who's in it."

She knew Billy wasn't trying to get one up her, but the caveman approach made her bridle.

Don't let fear guide you. You can't control everything.

That's what she'd told herself after *that night*. The night her blind trust in Eric had exploded into painful emotional shrapnel.

It was years ago. Move on. Not everyone was judging her. Billy didn't even know about her…her *situation*…so…

It was time to stop tarring everyone with the same brush.

They both pitched toward the right side of the ambulance as another wave bashed the side of the boat.

What the heck was happening out there? Armageddon?

Doing her best to not freak the children out, she tried appealing to Billy's macho side. "Go on, Billy. Be a hero and find out what's going on." She threw in a lame, "It's my name on the paperwork," then wiggled her phone between them as if that settled the matter.

The truth? They did need to find out what was happening and she wasn't sure her sea legs were up to whatever was happening out there. Besides, if something truly bad was going on, she needed a plan to get the children off the ferry, stat. No way was she losing them or exacerbating their critical injuries. Not when they'd already dodged the entrance to death's door a little less than a week ago.

Billy threw the radio cables onto the passenger seat of the front cab. "You know what I think?"

No. And judging by the narky tone of Billy's voice she didn't want to.

"I think someone wants first dibs on the boss man."

"Ha! Hardly."

She waited for him to get out of the ambo before she let her *yeah, right* face drop.

Okay. *Totally.* But it wasn't a factor right now. In an *emergency*.

She only did crushes from a distance. The second she stepped on to Maple Island? It would be work only.

Besides, her "crush" was nothing more than professional admiration.

Dr. Alex Kirkland was the answer to her prayers, *professionally*.

She was good at her job and working for Alex would only make her better. Not that she'd even spoken to him yet. She'd been hired by the clinic's co-founder, Cody Brennan, when he'd been over visiting a post-op patient she had been treating at Boston Harbor.

This was the chance of a lifetime and she wasn't going to let her poor taste in boyfriends destroy her future. It had taken three long years to build herself back up again after what Eric had done to her and no way was she going to let his arrival back in Boston push her back to that soul-destroying emotional precipice again.

She thumbed through her phone, barely catching her balance as the ferry reacted to another impact. There were high screeching sounds this time. The unmistakable scream of metal on rock.

Her heart dropped to her knees. Her badly bruised knees.

Didn't matter.

Maggie did another quick check of Peyton and Connor's stats. All good, despite the fact that being bounced around like this wasn't strictly on the rehab list. Just as well she and Billy had agreed to keep the children strapped into the ambulance instead of stretchering them onto the semi-exposed passenger desk as one officious cost-cutting administrator at Boston Harbor Hospital had suggested. Er...anyone ever heard of patient safety? She might be a goofball on any number of fronts, but patient welfare was definitely not one of them.

"You two all right?" She received a pair of dopey smiles. The painkillers were obviously doing their job. Excellent. The last thing she wanted was to add fear to the mix.

A crisp, efficient male voice answered the ringing phone with the name of the clinic.

"Hello? It's Maggie Green here from Boston Harbor. May I speak with Dr. Kirkland please?"

"This is he."

An unexpected trill of anticipation twirled around her heart and squeezed it tight. Alex Kirkland was legendary when it came to rehabilitation. His clinic. His terms. The place was a wonderland for a dedicated rehab physio. A job there was a true professional coup.

And a great place to hide away from ex-boyfriends.

The ferry came to a sudden halt then just as quickly felt like it was falling backwards. She yelped and braced herself to avoid falling on the children.

"Is everything all right?" he asked.

She wanted to say yes. She wanted to say everything was on track. Instead...she was going to have to set aside her deep-seated instinct not to ask for help.

"Not really. I'm on the ferry with the Walsh twins and—*Whoa!*"

Alex's voice clicked into the type of quick, professional tone an emergency operator would use. He was calm, assuring. "Maggie, can you still hear me? Are you with the children now?"

"Yes."

"Are they all right?"

"Yes. We're on the ferry as scheduled. Dr. Valdez got us all sorted at the docks, but it— Oops!"

Her hands flew out to brace herself and in the process knocked a supplies basket off the wall. She arched her body so the small boxes of gauze would fall on her and not Connor. The last thing he needed was more things falling on him.

"Maggie, where is Dr. Valdez now?"

She inched her way back to her seat and buckled herself in again.

"He had to stay in Boston to do an emergency surgery. The children are fine, but a fierce storm's blown in unexpectedly and the ferry seems to have run into some trouble."

The back door to the ambo flew open, along with a huge gust of wintry air. It was Billy. His features had turned ashen. "We've hit a rock. A big huge—"

Maggie drew a line across her throat and pointed at the children. She mimed closing the door as she tried to keep her voice steady. "We appear to have had a bit of a collision." As she watched Billy struggle to close the doors behind him, her mind reeled with ways to get the children off safely. The wind was obviously too strong for a helicopter. Not to mention that their clear day had turned into one with zero visibility. They must be halfway between Boston and Maple Island. Only half an hour on a good day. On a bad one? She didn't have a clue.

The ferry was being bashed around by the waves so there wasn't a chance in the universe the tiny lifeboats would be of any use. Unless they were sinking.

Oh, jeezy-peeps. They'd better not be sinking.

"Can you send anyone to fetch us? We might be in somewhat of a pickle here." The biggest type of pickle, actually. The life-or-death kind if this was going the way she feared. Maggie bit down on the inside of her cheek so hard she drew blood.

"Leave it with me." Alex's rich southern voice was exactly the solid reassurance she needed to hear. "Your priority is the children." Then the phone went dead.

She stared at the phone. The man certainly wasn't one for small talk.

Right now isn't the time for pleasantries, you idiot!

Besides, he was ex-military, wasn't he? All the doctors she'd worked with who had served were more about action than chitchat.

"You two twin berries all right?" Maggie started taking everything down from the sides of the ambulance that could fall, doing her best to sound calm when everything inside her was freaking right the heck out of Dodge. Chances were they were going to have to get out of the ambulance asap.

An obstetrics kit fell off its wall hook. She grabbed it just in time.

Don't panic. Don't panic.

She swept a lock of black hair away from Peyton's face with one of her rainbow-color painted nails. "How you holding up there, hon? You okay?"

The ten-year-old was looking pretty pale, but then again blunt trauma to her spinal column was no laughing matter. Neither was the resulting Brown-Sequard syndrome. The rare spinal injury could have been deadly. A wooden shard from the scaffolding that had collapsed on her and her brother had pierced her spinal cord, triggering the neurological response. Dr. Valdez had stopped the spinal fluid from leaking and, whilst she still was experiencing some numbness and sensory loss, it looked as though she would not suffer permanent paralysis.

The minor fractures she'd received to her spinal column? Well. Time and a positive attitude were going to be both the twins' best friends for the next few months. An amazing surgeon from Spain had helped, too. And not sinking in an ambulance on a ferryboat just off the coast of Boston? That would also be a factor.

She pinned on a smile. "It looks like New Year's Day is a bit more wild than we thought."

"I'm okay if Connor's okay," Peyton whispered.

Boom!

This time it was Maggie's heart that took the blow. These two kids. They tugged at just about every single one of her heartstrings. She'd been in the hospital when the twins had been brought in on Christmas Eve.

A few days later, once she'd connected the dots—low-income backgrounds, parents embroiled in a legal tangle with a reluctant insurance company, the charitable offer from the Maple Island Clinic to cover the long-term rehab—she'd realized they were headed for the same place and had volunteered to oversee the transfer to the island when Dr. Valdez wasn't able to make it, even though it meant she'd arrive a week earlier than she'd been contracted for.

Not that it was the best excuse in the universe to get out of Boston fast.

She gave Connor's dark hair a gentle scrub. He'd also taken a severe blow from the scaffolding, but at least he'd missed out on getting a spinal puncture wound from the splintered beams that had shattered when the scaffolding clamps had given way. Peyton had really taken the brunt of this one.

Their recovery after surgery at Boston Harbor had been one of those "wait and see" issues. Never nice for the patient. More traumatizing for the parents.

Her own parents had just about had a meltdown when… well… They'd eventually got over it and she was getting on just fine now. All things considered.

She smiled down at Connor. "You all right, bud?"

"Wicked cool." Connor gave her a double thumbs-up, even though his arms were strapped down along with the rest of his body. Any sort of movement could compromise the exacting surgery he'd just had. She gave herself a fist bump within his eyeline then returned his thumbs-up.

How was she going to get these kids safely off this boat?

The ferry shifted and groaned again. Her insides went liquid with fear. Was this their *Titanic* moment?

"All good, kiddos. Everything's okay," she lied. "Thank goodness you two are strapped in, right?"

They probably ought to get them out of the ambo and upstairs, where they stood a better chance of not being sucked into the icy Atlantic waters, but…with the ferry moving around so much, what if they dropped them?

It'd be like walking around with unpinned, kid-shaped grenades.

She shot Billy a look. One she hoped asked, *Any bright ideas?*

Billy mouthed something about finding the crew and climbed out of the ambo with another gush of wintry wind.

In a vain attempt to make this seem fun and not terrifying, Maggie took two big fistfuls of her flame-red hair and held them out whilst making a goofy face.

Total failure.

At ten years old, Peyton and Connor were old enough to roll their eyes at adults trying to be cool and still young enough to be scared.

"You two hold steady there." Maggie winced. As if they had a choice. She knew more than most how hard it was to be told not to worry when the only option was to rely on other people.

"Maybe you should call Dad." Peyton's eyes were still red-rimmed from the emotional farewell with their parents at the hospital.

"That's a great idea, Pey." Maggie cherry-picked the information that would scare them least. "We'll send him a text, but I'm pretty sure he's at work." She didn't think. She knew. Both he and Mrs. Walsh had been told by their employers that if they didn't show up to work, they would lose their jobs. This on top of their insurance company's refusal to pay out. As if the Walshes had been the ones to will the arctic winter winds to blow both the house's porch scaffolding and the porch onto their children on Christmas Eve.

They might be poor, but the last thing the Walshes were was negligent.

"Maybe a helicopter will come rescue us," Connor suggested.

Maggie made an "Ooh" noise, followed by an *I don't think that's gonna happen* frown.

"The weather isn't good enough for a helicopter to fly in, dummy," Peyton snapped at her brother.

At least Peyton was feeling good enough to name-call. It was when fear became silence and then silence became acceptance that it swallowed you whole. Maggie had fought that battle thousands of times in her own life and had found that smiling at adversity really was the best way to deal with life's challenges.

Right. Operation Positive Thinking!

"We're going to be fine. Probably just stopping for a pod of harbor seals or something."

"It's a pod of *whales*. Seals are bob, harem, colony or rookery. Besides, the harbor seals don't come round the cape in winter. It's harp and hooded seals in January."

"Well, that's very interesting, Connor. What else do you know about seals?" Distractions. Perfect. Maggie put on her best interested face as Vicky jumped into the front cab of the ambulance, along with a howl of wind.

"Is the ferry sinking?" Peyton's hands strained against the straps holding her onto her tray gurney.

"Ha! No." Maggie threw a quick *Will it?* look at Vicky, whose return expression wasn't very reassuring. "It won't sink. Even if it does, you're with a hydrotherapist. Perfect person to be with."

The ferry lurched again. This time it was obvious the boat was tipping in the wrong direction.

Don't panic. Don't panic.

"I thought your therapy used horses, not water." Connor's voice wobbled as he spoke. "You said we could ride with you one day."

"Absolutely. We will ride together and swim together. I do all sorts of different things." Including screw up her life so much she ended up on a sinking ferry on New Year's Day with two kids who seriously deserved a break but who weren't getting one.

Adrenaline was normally her friend. She was going to have to make it her best friend today.

"Lay it on me, Vick," she whispered out of the children's earshot. "What's going on?"

Vicky grabbed a couple of reflective vests out of the glove compartment and turned to her, looking utterly terrified. "Billy's helping with the lifeboats. We need to get the kids out of here right now."

No news was good news.

That's what Alex was telling himself anyway. He stared at the phone again. Twenty attempted calls and each time it had cut out.

No news is good news.

When it involved a sinking ferry? No news could be the worst possible kind of news.

He'd already had enough of that in his life, thank you very much.

He pulled off his woolen hat and gave his sandy blond hair a scrub. Every nerve ending in his body was crackling with barely contained frustration. If jumping into the sea and swimming would have got them through the storm faster, he would've done it.

The urge surprised him. Particularly given the barely disguised nickname he knew his staff had for him.

Dr. Protocol.

His fingers tightened round the brass railing in the small enclosed helm area Salty kept in immaculate condition.

There were rules for a reason.

Rules Mother Nature didn't feel inclined to pay much attention to.

It was insane to be out in this weather at all. He had a young son to look after. A clinic to run.

She needs your help.

They *all* needed his help.

He pushed the thoughts away. This wasn't some magic chance for him to leap in and change history. His wife had been killed in action. There hadn't been a single thing he could've done about it.

She could've followed orders and she'd still be alive.

His preference of fact over the futility of what-might-have-been laid the argument to rest. What's done was done.

Right here, right now? He had patients who needed his help and Maggie Green had better be following emergency guidelines to a T.

He looked across at Old Salty, the island's resident commercial fisherman who had volunteered to bring him out here. His last name was Harrington. Alex had never learned his first. All the islanders called him by his nickname, so he did, too.

The septuagenarian's piercing blue eyes popped out beneath the navy captain's hat he near enough always wore. A snow-white beard. Bit of a pot belly. He'd look like a nautical Santa if he wasn't so damn grumpy all the time. Then again, there weren't all that many folk willing to risk it all for a pair of young patients stranded on a sinking ferry off Boston Harbor. The man was made of the stern stuff of previous generations. The type who actually *had* walked to school through three feet of snow.

In fairness, Maple Island virtually overflowed with helping hands when needed. It was a proper community looking after its own. It was one of the reasons he and Cody had picked it for the clinic.

Three years he'd been on the island now. Given the fact the island was home to descendants of the *Mayflower*, he didn't know if he'd ever feel anything other than brand new.

But he knew he'd stay. He felt welcome. And that made all the difference.

Didn't mean the learning curve wasn't steep. Cody was from California and Alex was from Alabama. A New England storm was still about as foreign to the pair of them as calling a place home for over two hundred years. And with temperatures below freezing, snow predicted and winds howling in from the Arctic Circle he was in completely new territory.

"It was good of Marlee to get in touch with you."

"She didn't," Salty said.

Alex gave him a sidelong look. He obviously wasn't going to offer up any more information.

Marlee was one of the clinic's biggest assets and he wasn't just talking about her bear hugs. If she wasn't related to someone who could help, she'd gone to kindergarten with them, or had baked cookies with them or had raised her kids with them. The instant she sniffed trouble, she went into turbo drive and before he'd pulled on his first layer of thermals Alex had found himself being bundled into a four-by-four en route to the harbor, along with a set of thick waterproofs. When they'd arrived, Old Salty had already been untying his fishing boat's thick bow lines off the dockside cleats.

"Should be any minute now." Salty squinted into the mist, not an ounce of concern about him.

How did he do that? There was a broken-down ferry, possibly taking on water. Two patients on board who should already be in the clinic's small but up-to-date intensive care unit. And a new employee he had absolutely no information about. Cody had handled the interviews with her so he had no information on what she'd be like. Scared. Capable. Bewildered. Dead?

His phone buzzed. Cody. His human wall to bounce ideas off. Half the time he never knew if Cody was even listening to him. The other half? He'd never met a smarter, more committed surgeon in his life. Two single dads doing their best to bring their children up in a world they never thought they'd be navigating alone.

Or, as Cody had pronounced when they'd finalized their building plans, "Life's a bitch, and then you build a clinic."

"Any news on your end, Cody?"

He heard a slapping sound. No doubt Cody's hand against the counter. Frustration was definitely getting the better of both of them. "No. I was hoping you'd have some. Hey, listen, there's something I need to warn you about Maggie—"

The line cut out.

Alex stared at the phone. What did he mean? Way to end on a cliff hanger.

"Look over there, boy," Salty ordered.

Boy?

Alex bit back a mirthless laugh. It had gotten a bit too much use of late.

He hadn't been a boy let alone *felt* like one since...far too long.

No point in pretending he couldn't remember. The last time he'd felt properly young had been the moment he'd fallen in love with his wife. And that had been a long time ago. Best-looking woman in boot camp. Smartest, too. Had known her way round combat medicine as if she'd been born on a battlefield. A heart the size of the whole of New York City. Six years after her death, and he still struggled to believe someone so vital had been snuffed out in an instant. That was the only mercy. She'd never seen it coming.

"You can just make them out there."

He tugged his wool hat back on and followed the line of Salty's thick finger as he pointed toward a dark object in the distance largely obscured by the murky weather.

"Got it. Let's get those children on board this boat and get them back to the clinic before anything else goes wrong."

CHAPTER TWO

DOCKING A BOAT to an engine-less ferry perched on a jagged rocky outcrop in the midst of a winter storm was no mean feat. It wasn't sinking at the moment—but it certainly wasn't sitting at an angle that was going to hold for much longer if the waves grew any fiercer.

With each surge and lift of the fishing boat he could see the ambulance. He'd half expected to see it on its side, doors flapping and a whole lot of other things that weren't very pleasant.

It was upright and solidly strapped to various posts by four thick docking ropes. Someone was a clever-clogs.

"Right, boy. That's the *Flying Cod* cinched in. You want to get these little 'uns on board and back to the island?" Salty nodded at the rope ladder one of the ferry's crew had just flung their way.

"Absolutely."

Alex pulled himself up and over the railing and ran. He only just managed to pull himself to a halt as the double doors at the back of the ambulance swung open.

The storm, the high-octane adrenaline that came with the insane rescue mission, Old Salty's salty language… none of it had the impact she did.

Hair like spun gold and flames. The biggest pair of brown eyes he'd ever seen. There were probably flecks of gold in them if the light was right. Pitch-black lashes giving them that added visual punch. Cheeks pinked up with the cold or…hell, he didn't know why a woman's cheeks pinked up. All he knew was that he'd better get some oxygen back into his lungs so he could speak.

She had a rope on her shoulder coiled up like a lasso.

"Hope that's not for me."

Kicking himself would be a good option about now.

She gave him a sideways look and a quick up-down scan. "Could be if you play your cards right."

Was he—? Were they—?

This wasn't *flirting*, was it?

"We should get a move on."

Nice one, Alex. Way to roll out the charm.

"Absolutely." She gave him a bright smile. "We probably need all hands on deck—like a human chain—in case the sea goes all bouncy-bouncy on us again. Although that's why we put up the guide lines." They both turned and looked at the ropes holding the ambulance in place. He saw now that there were more ropes tied at a higher level, serving as hand grips.

"You did this?"

She shrugged as if tying a vehicle with two extremely injured children inside of it during a freak winter storm was an everyday sort of thing for her. "With help from the ambo team and the ferry crew. You're Dr. Kirkland, right? Maggie Green."

She put out a hand.

He ignored it.

There'd only been one other woman who'd suckerpunched him into sensory overload quite so fast and the only place he could visit her was at her graveside.

Maggie's eyes narrowed slightly, as if trying to get the measure of him. She withdrew her hand and gave him a nod in a way that suggested she saw him for what he was. A man at war with himself.

That made a change. Most people thought he was an

uptight stick-in-the-mud. Rules. Regulations. The world's most boring man.

He wasn't that guy.

He hadn't been, at least.

"All right, doc?" Billy appeared from around the corner, pulling on a reflective waterproof with the Boston Harbor logo sewn onto the front.

A wave bashed the side of the ferry and threw them all off balance. Maggie fell forward from her perch in the ambulance door. Alex lunged forward, just managing to keep the pair of them upright.

His breath caught as she steadied herself, using his chest as an anchor. It was the first time he'd ever been grateful to be wearing five layers of clothes. Her hand on his bare chest? Just thinking about it shot his temperature up to the stratosphere.

Her eyes widened as they met his. A hot, intense connection froze the pair of them in place.

"You all right, you two?" Billy stepped forward.

As quickly as she'd fallen, Maggie pulled herself back into the ambulance doorway.

What the hell just happened there?

"Right." Alex needlessly clapped his hands together. There was hardly a cast of thousands standing at attention. "Everyone we need here?"

Billy nodded. "Vicky, me, and Maggie, of course."

As if he wasn't aware of the flame-haired beauty who'd burst out of the ambulance like a film starlet ready to take the world by storm.

Billy pointed toward Salty's boat. "There're a couple of ferry crew over there by your fishing boat. Should be enough. A few passengers upstairs if we need 'em, but I would say they're more hungover than helpful. We'll take your lead."

Alex's years in the military kicked to the fore. He walked with Vicky and Billy toward Salty's boat, issuing sharp, exacting instructions about how they'd load the twins onto the vessel using Maggie's pre-established guidelines. He knew he sounded curt, like an automaton, but it helped blinker his thoughts. Right up until Maggie jumped down out of the cab and walked toward him. She was all legs and then some. From the tips of her high-profile athletic shoes to the farthest reach of her sprawl of flame-colored curls, she moved like a cross between a jungle cat and a supermodel, as if walking along an unsteady ferry deck with a storm raging around her was the most natural thing in the world.

"Dr. Kirkland? Where do you want me?"

All sorts of places it wouldn't be appropriate to go into right now.

He shook his head. He felt like he was being invaded by an Alex he had never met before. One part Viking and one part Don Juan. In other words, one hundred percent opposite from the man he needed to be right now.

"Dr. Kirkland?" Maggie held up her hands and gave her fingers a wiggle. "Where do you want them and what do you want them doing?"

An explicit image of Maggie raking her colorful nails down his naked back blindsided him.

Her presence was more than distracting. She was lighting up all sorts of primal sensors he'd long thought were dead. Sparks and shocks were crackling against his insides as if someone was trying to start up an ice-cold truck in his privates.

He pulled off his hat again and scrubbed his hands through his hair. Half of him wanted to send her back to Boston on the bright yellow rescue boat he could see approaching at the far end of the ferry. The other half? He crushed the thoughts into the darkest corner of his brain he could find. He'd deal with that later.

"Stay with the ambo. We'll sort out the swiftest transfer method and let you know when we need you."

She pushed herself up to her full height, eyes flashing with something he couldn't put a name to. Anger? Frustration?

"Listen here, Mr. Southern Drawl. That cute little accent and sexy hero act of yours isn't going to work on me. I'm here to help, not stand around and look pretty."

She did that all right. Without even trying.

Wait a minute. *Sexy hero?* Hardly. Work-focused single dad with about as much fun in his entire body as Maggie looked to have in her pinkie finger would be a better description. And a "cute" accent? Where he came from, all his accent did was ensure everyone knew he was from the wrong side of the tracks. It was why he'd joined the military. Which side of the tracks a person came from didn't hold much sway on a battlefield.

Alex cleared his throat and readjusted his stance to that of commanding officer—a role he'd relinquished the day his wife had been killed. "Precisely why I need you to stay at the ambo. We're loading the patients one by one. At my clinic we don't leave juvenile, post-operative spinal injury patients on their own."

What the—? Who'd drained his personality and refilled him with formaldehyde?

Maggie's dismissive shrug confirmed she didn't think much of his behavior either. "I wasn't planning on abandoning them. And in my world? We call patients by their *names*. They have them, you know. Peyton and Connor Walsh. They're *kids*. And they're scared. Might be a good idea to come over here and introduce yourself before you carry on barking orders at everyone."

Irritation flared in him hot and bright. He took patient care immensely seriously. He'd set up the clinic with the highest of standards for precisely that reason, and here she was giving him *How to Treat a Patient for Beginners* tips.

She was right, of course. Infuriating. But right.

"Hello…" Maggie waved a hand in front of his face. "Anybody home?"

Alex frowned. "There is a procedure to be followed. Chitchat can come later."

"Wow." Maggie didn't even try to hide her distaste at his response.

He held up a hand and started ticking off questions on his fingers. "Have you checked on their life vests? The cover for transport? The waterproofing. The transfer protocol?"

"Obviously. We kind of saw to that when the ferry smashed into the rocks and we all thought we might drown." She stared at him for a moment then started to laugh. "Omigawd! I didn't put two and two together, but you're *him*."

"Who?" He was her boss, for one. That should be clear enough. His name was stitched onto his jacket. Made it easy to identify staff in moments of chaos. Just like this one.

"Dr. Protocol."

He winced. Nice to know his reputation for exacting adherence to procedure had preceded him.

"Sorry. Sorry. That was meant to be my inside voice." She teased her shoulders into performing an impish shrug of apology to match her rueful *I really messed that up* face.

Alex gritted his teeth.

She quirked an eyebrow at him.

I'm waiting, it said. And a whole lot more.

Everything about Maggie Green spoke to that perfect triple of determination, energy, and willingness to take risks. That sort of optimism wasn't something you learned. It was something a person *embodied*. And Maggie positively glowed with it. A stark contrast to the cloud he was pretty sure shadowed him on most days.

In other words, if he was the phoenix burned to ashes, she was all flame.

Exactly the type of person they needed working with patients teetering on the ledge between despair and recovery.

Annoyingly.

The idea of three months working with Maggie Green was settling in about as easily as he'd taken to the mandatory grief counseling after Amy had been killed. Very. Poorly.

Maggie looked at him for a minute, arms crossed, jaw twitching with expectation. "C'mon, Dr. Kirkland. Come say hi."

She turned without waiting for a response, those long legs of hers taking the few yards between him and the ambulance in a handful of strides. She turned around and crooked her arm, a smile teasing at the corners of her mouth as she beckoned him to join her. "I promise they don't bite."

Then she winked at him.

CHAPTER THREE

MAGGIE CLAMBERED INTO the back of the ambulance hoping her expression read more *Hey, kids! We're about to have an adventure* rather than the more horrifying alternative.

Had she really just *winked* at her new boss?

How completely and totally mortifying.

She wasn't a winker. She wasn't even a flirt. And yet just five seconds in Alex Kirkland's presence and for some insane reason she'd thought she'd had a little glimpse into his soul. Seen a kindred spirit. Which was completely insane. Bring on the straitjacket! Maggie Green's finally lost the plot!

If only his gorgeous southern accent hadn't wriggled its way down her spine the way it had. The man wasn't just sexy. Less than a handful of seconds in his arms and he'd dug up all sorts of sensations she hadn't banked on feeling ever again. Since when did she get all tingly in her fastidiously padlocked *magic garden*?

Mercifully, Vicky stuck her head into the back of the ambulance instead of Alex and the proverbial ball started rolling.

Twenty hair-raising minutes later the impressive seadog manning the fishing boat was pulling up to a classic old-fashioned marina on Maple Island. The tide was high and docking was no easy feat as the waves kept were bashing up against the fishing vessel.

Despite the relative silence in which they had traveled back to the island, she was as aware of Alex Kirkland as he seemed to be of her.

Which was why focusing solely on her charges had made the bumpy journey easier. The last thing she needed was to be going all doe-eyed on her new boss. She didn't do romantic relationships. Not even for cantankerous, butterfly-inducing, green-eyed procedure devotees whose delicious personal man scent was now embossed on her memory...forever.

If they could bottle Eau d'Alex Kirkland? The patient load at Maple Clinic would double. Overnight. Not that he seemed like the kind of guy who liked a fan club. Quite the opposite, in fact. When she'd accidentally winked at him he'd looked as though he'd have fled for the hills if they hadn't been on a boat.

A handful of men and women all wearing thick winter coats with the Maple Island Clinic logo embossed on them were at the docks. Alex jumped out first and rattled off a few instructions. That seemed to be his thing. But something told her he was doing it now because he was unsettled. And it wasn't the patients who'd been doing the unsettling.

Whatever. She was used to being the elephant in the room.

She was also used to bringing out the worst in people. It was her thing. With patients she could wrestle the fury into submission. With Eric? It had nearly crushed her, but she'd found a way to get back up again. Swinging.

Whatever it was she'd unzipped in Alex, suffice it to say he wasn't the only one feeling unsettled.

"Are you sure you and Salty can manage from your end?"

Alex's green eyes pierced straight through to the one area of her confidence she'd thought unshakable. Her ability to follow through physically. It wasn't as if she had dedicated her whole life to being "capable" or anything.

"Absolutely." She threw her cockiest smile back at him. "So long as you and your posse are up to being on the receiving end of our superpowers." She turned to Salty. "You up for throwing some shade on the clinic crew dockside?"

Salty frowned. "I have no idea what you're saying, girlie, but let's get these young 'uns up onto the pier and out of the weather."

Maggie laughed good-naturedly and moved into position at the end of Connor's stretcher. The ride hadn't exactly been a barrel of laughs but they'd made it. If Alex's predictions were anything to go by, in just a few more minutes they'd be nice and warm in the clinic's A-grade facilities. She strongly suspected Alex's predictions were fact-based and nothing less.

She looked up at him from her end of the stretcher and tried not to blink as their eyes met and locked.

She knew then and there that he was going to expect the very best from her. Exactly what she was hoping for professionally. Personally? Not so much.

"Miss Green? Any time now."

"Yup! On it." She squatted into place, hoping no one called Alex saw her suck in a sharp breath as her knees registered their complaints. She could practically feel his eyes glued to her. The man was unnerving her. Putting her off her game.

Enough with the excuses. Just get on with it.

"All right, Connor. You ready?" The boy gave them a thumbs-up and sucked in a big inhalation of wintry sea air as Salty and Maggie bent and hoisted his stretcher up and toward the pairs of hands waiting on the dock.

The hands that accepted her end of the stretcher brushed against hers. Electric sparks skittered down her arm and swirled round her chest before floating provocatively down to that freshly unlocked secret place of hers.

No guesses as to who had taken her end of the stretcher. She didn't dare look at Alex again. Instead she focused on getting Peyton up and into the back of the waiting four-by-four. As she turned on the boat's crowded deck, her foot caught and snagged on a rope, giving her knee a painful wrench.

Ooh, that hurt. Really, really, really hurt. It's all right. You can take it. Just a few more minutes and then you'll be taking a load off.

"You gonna stand there daydreaming or are you going to help me get this girlie onto the dock?"

"Right! Sorry, Salty. Can I call you Salty?"

He leant to pick up his end of the stretcher in tandem with her. "It's 'may', not 'can.' And I don't see why not. Everyone else does."

Ha. Well, that had put her in her place. "Is there something else you'd rather be called?"

His blue eyes flashed brightly. "Nope." He lifted his end of the stretcher with a bit of a grunt that could easily have been described as a growl.

There was definitely a story there. One she'd have to get before her contract was up.

"We've got her."

"Hang on a minute," Salty called out to the clinic staffers, who were already heading to the transport vehicles. "Still got these bags for this little lady to load up."

"Oh, don't worry about those, Salty. I'll get them." Maggie waved for the medics with the twins to go on ahead as she tried to wrestle her duffel bag away from Salty.

Precious cargo. She was a bit touchy about them. Especially with the boat still bucking around like it was. Proof, if they'd needed any, that Salty's seasoned negotiation of the ocean to the ferry and safely back to the island again had been a feat in and of itself.

"It's no trouble," He put one leg on the dock and one on the boat. The man was pretty nimble for a self-proclaimed "old feller." He flicked his fingers, indicating she should hand him her large duffels that the ambo crew had kindly jammed into the front cab with them, which she did. "What in the blue blazes have you got in here, woman? A dead body?"

She laughed. Near enough. "I don't travel light."

That'd cover her bases for now. He wasn't to know. No one was until she was ready to tell them. She never liked to make her condition "a thing" until it became…a thing.

"Oh, for the love of—!"

With the bash of a wave came an abrupt swing and shift of the boat against the dock. Salty tried, unsuccessfully to find purchase on the dockside but couldn't. His "boat" leg slipped between the vessel and the dock and the rest of his body flew forward so rapidly his hands were unable to brace him for the fall. Adrenaline took over as she leapt to Salty's aid.

Gritting her teeth against her own pain, Maggie managed to climb out of the boat and pull his leg up and onto the dock. She told herself to call for help, but wasn't entirely sure if she had the breath in her lungs to shout.

"Salty? Salty." She knelt next to him and pressed her fingers to the pulse point on his throat. Thready. But still there. "Come on, you old seadog. You aren't going to let a little old storm get the better of you, are you? Certainly not on New Year's Day, all right?"

Her eyes flicked to his torn yellow coveralls that were now exposing a navy pants leg. She couldn't see any blood coming through, but the fabric was both dark and wet, so not the easiest way to see it. If he'd suffered a compound fracture the wound would need to be cleaned as soon as possible. Infection was an open wound's biggest enemy.

Other people appeared then began calling out for more help, a stretcher, blankets, a doctor. Salty kept blinking his blue eyes as though they were trying to bring her into focus. From the look of the bump on his head he could've easily suffered a concussion too.

She pulled off her jacket, took off her fleece and curled it round his head like a cushion. "Salty? Can you follow my finger?" She clocked his eye movement as they followed her index finger. It wasn't brilliant but it wasn't bad. To distract him from what must be an excruciating level of pain, she kept up her usual bright chatter and carried on performing the handful of neurological exams easily performed on a recumbent patient.

When the clamor of voices fell silent she knew whose body was attached to the solid all-weather boots that appeared in her sightline.

Alex Kirkland.

Much to Maggie's surprise, Salty tried to push himself up to a sitting position. "Just let me get up, would you? Give me a chance to have a quick run down the dock on it. A couple of laps and it'll be fine."

Maggie pushed him back down. "Let's just hang onto that enthusiasm for a minute, Salty."

Calmly, steadily, Alex swiftly examined Salty's leg.

Maggie knew she was holding her breath, but she also knew how bad the injury could be. Soft tissue damage alone could lead to amputation. It had been difficult to tell just how violent a blow Salty's leg had received, but popliteal artery injury was something to consider. Compartment syndrome. Or infections. *Please don't let him get an infection.* There was gangrene to consider, osteomyelitis—

Alex shot her a curious sidelong look. She hoped he wasn't reading her mind.

"I'm guessing we're looking at a double oblique fracture," he said. "Most likely tib and fib, but I don't want to destabilize it more than it already might be."

She exhaled. Okay. Better than completely crushed to smithereens.

"I'd rather leave any guesses on the ankle to the radiography team." The crowd around them collectively gasped as Alex's comments made the rounds. It sounded bad. It *was* bad. Alex maintained solid eye contact with Salty. "The good news is nothing's broken through, but you do present with one gross deformity."

Despite years of hearing the medical term, Maggie winced. She hated that term, "gross deformities." Whenever she was with patients she always made a joke of it and called them "beautiful variations." Being injured or in pain was bad enough. No need to add insult to an actual injury.

Alex shook his head as once again Salty tried to lift himself up. The old man gave a grunt of irritation and lay back down on the dock, his eyes closed tight as Alex continued, "We're most likely going to have to set the bones, Salty. A pretty good reason not to keep trying to get up and test it out." Maggie pressed her fingers to Salty's carotid artery. Irritation had ratcheted up his heart rate. Better than thready, but skyrocketing in the other direction wasn't great either.

Patiently, and presumably as a time-filler until more help could arrive, Alex continued, "Pending a follow through on any soft-tissue damage and splinting you, with any luck, and some proper physio from Maggie here, we'll have you up and running in a couple of months."

"Months?" Salty roared, eliciting a few shrieks from the onlookers who'd thought his closed eyes had meant he had passed out.

Maggie could barely hear her own voice trying to tell him an oblique fracture was a good thing such was the roar of blood careering round her own brain.

Broken was so much better than what she'd imagined.

"Chin up, Salty. You'll be back in action in no time," she told the old man.

Alex threw her A Look. "If by 'no time' you mean possibly having to go through surgery and attend months of rehab *after* the fractures have healed, I suppose you're right."

Alex's tone made his stance crystal clear. He didn't "do" optimism. He did facts.

Maggie's blood shot from ice cold straight up to boiling point. The facts weren't all in yet and optimism had helped her over more than a few hurdles in her life.

"Your bedside manner stinks," she ground out through gritted teeth.

"Both of yers does." Salty tried to push himself up once more, only to have Alex and Maggie press him back down onto the thick wooden dock planks. "Listen up, the pair of you," Salty persisted. "All I need is a good hot cup of coffee. One of Fiona's'll do. I don't want any cardamom or turmeric or any sort of nut milk anywhere near my cup of Joe. And I'm hungry so I'd a like a cruller to go with it. While I have that you can tape up my leg, then the both of you can get on over to the clinic so I can shut down the *Fish Tank* for the night."

"Erm… Salty?" Maggie shot a look at Alex, who was still very busy glaring at her. "I think the *Fish Tank* needs to be shut down for a bit longer than that. And perhaps by someone who isn't you. Do you have any family who can help?"

Salty's already murderous expression turned even darker. "Nope."

He folded his arms across his chest and stared at the steel-gray sky that was turning suspiciously darker by the minute.

Someone pushed through the crowd. "Utter rot and nonsense, Salty. You've got us, whether you're happy with it or not."

Salty shifted his eyes to stare at the new arrival. A man with a bright orange crew cut who could've doubled as a leprechaun. Brave, too, as he was wagging his finger at Salty as if he'd been a naughty toddler.

"Tom Brady, I hope you've got a cruller in one of those pockets of yours, otherwise I'm not remotely interested in what you're about to say."

"You know there are crullers on tap for you every day of the week at the bakery, Salty, but perhaps the doc here might like you to wait a couple of minutes. Now, I'll get Jim down here and he and I'll see to the *Fish Tank*." He nodded to Alex. "Dr. Kirkland. Good to see you, despite the circumstances. You and your son see in the New Year on your own?"

Alex nodded and gave the man's shoulder a quick affirmative clap. "I imagine the Brady family saw it in with their usual verve."

"I'll have a headache for days," Tom confirmed with a smile.

Alex laughed and shook his head.

Okay. So he wasn't Captain von Grumpy to everyone. Just her. If there was any sort of record being taken, she would like it duly noted that she found Dr. Alex Kirkland infuriatingly…he turned to her with a soft apologetic smile playing on those lips of his…*gorgeous*.

He looked back at Tom. "I think Salty could do with a couple of extra pairs of hands today."

"That's settled, then. I'll get the boys down and they'll clean her up."

"Not necessary!" Salty growled.

"Definitely necessary," said another man who looked an awful lot like Tom Brady. "From where I'm standing, you aren't looking your best."

That was one way to put it.

All the blood had drained from Salty's face. His breath was coming in quick, sharp huffs. The body's way of coping with pain. If they didn't get him somewhere dry and warm soon they could add hypothermia to his list.

As if by magic, a woman in a Maple Island Clinic jacket appeared with a backboard.

"Can we get a bit of space around Salty, please, folks?" Alex ordered. "Just need to load him up and get him to the clinic."

"I don't know what my insurance is going to think of this," Salty bit out.

"Doesn't matter," Alex said matter-of-factly. "You were doing a clinic rescue mission. All your care is on us."

A shot of respect crackled along Maggie's spine. Gorgeous and with ramrod-straight integrity. She sniffed. Didn't mean his social skills couldn't do with some improvement, but everyone had their crosses to bear.

Salty grumbled but didn't resist.

Then Alex started reciting another list of instructions so specific she had to hide her smile.

Dr. Protocol, indeed.

He was obviously a good doctor. His neurosurgical skills were highly lauded in all the articles she'd read about him before she'd taken the three-month contract at the clinic. Ground-breaking this and new innovations that. She'd had run-ins with a lot of surgeons in her time. They could be elitist. Reserved. Brusque. Downright rude. Alex obviously had the brains, but now that she'd watched him interact with Salty and the other islanders who were still pitching in as if this sort of thing happened every day, she realized he also had compassion. And that was a game changer as far as she was concerned. Anyone who could put themselves in someone else's shoes...

This was going to be a funny few months. Whether it was going to be funny ha-ha or funny peculiar remained to be seen.

CHAPTER FOUR

"Neurovascular assessment borderline."

"Borderline?" Alex took off his coat as he listened to Dr. Cody Brennan reel off his findings.

"The swelling has obviously interfered with certain results. His blood pressure's all over the place. We've set Mr. Harrington—"

"Salty?"

Cody shot him a quick look. "Yes. That's what I said. Mr. Harrington. Salty. Same thing. We've set his leg in a soft cast and put him on a drip. The swelling on his head appears to be superficial. Long and short of it? He won't need surgery." Cody was staring at his ever-present tablet as he spoke, and Alex knew him well enough by now that that was probably all the information he'd be getting from his colleague.

As a respected orthopedic surgeon, Alex was more than happy to take Cody's word for it.

Co-founding the clinic with him had been just about one of the best things he'd done since his wife had died. Not double checking on exactly who they were hiring when Cody had told him he'd brought on another physio was not.

For a number of reasons.

Some were practical. Maggie Green clearly sang from a very different hymnbook when it came to health and safety. Not that he could poke holes in how she'd handled today's extreme situation, but…

Fine. She unnerved him. Her…her looks. Those dusky rose lips of hers. That smile that seemed to light up her face from the outside in. She oozed *life*.

"She's the best in her game."

"Who?"

"Maggie. So quit looking like I poured salt in your coffee. She's staying."

Alex stared at Cody. "I didn't say one thing about Maggie."

"You didn't have to," Cody said dryly, finally looking up from his tablet. "You're acting funny."

Alex just managed to stop himself from retorting, "Am not."

He was a grown man. He ran a world-class clinic. He did not engage in schoolyard imbroglios over whether or not he had a crush on the new girl.

He fixed Cody with his best grown-up face.

"I presume you've got Rosaline on the case?" The Haitian nurse who'd agreed to work over the holiday period was a no-nonsense stickler. Tough enough to take Salty's complaints—which were accruing by the minute—on the chin.

"Yup." Cody was already wandering off, lost, no doubt, in the details of another patient's upcoming surgery. If the weather was anything to go by, he'd be stuck doing the minor surgeries here on the island rather than the more high-stakes surgeries he performed over at Boston Harbor. Alex made a mental to note to charge himself with hiring the next physio. He also needed to put a call in to Dr. Rafael Valdez and commend him on the excellent work he'd done with the twins. They could do with a surgeon of his caliber on staff. He wondered if Rafael would ever consider—

"Um…excuse me."

Alex felt a tap on his shoulder but didn't need to turn

around to know who it was. The combination of the smoky voice and citrus scent spoke for her. Maggie Green.

"Yes? How can I help?" He turned and took a couple of steps back. Close proximity to Maggie was…unsettling.

"Yeah…er…" Her dark eyes shot up to the right as she continued, "This is a little bit awkward, but is there any chance someone could show me to my living quarters? I should probably get a shower."

Alex narrowed his eyes and scanned her. His response came out in staccato observations.

"Your lips are blue."

"They're just a little cold after the day out and Salty was using my fleece as a pillow, so—"

"There's a bump on your forehead."

Her slender fingers flew to touch it and when she made contact she drew in a sharp breath. "I'd forgotten about that. Nothing to worry about. Just took a bit of a conk when the children and I were in the ambulance. I'd love to see them, but maybe when I'm looking a bit less like a zombie?" She grimaced and gave her chilled arms a rub.

"Why haven't you been shown your room yet?"

She grinned. "I'm guessing it might have something to do with young patients arriving in less than ordinary circumstances on a holiday, chased up by the hero of the day getting a double fracture? Plus the fact I'm a week early for work." She lifted her eyebrows when he said nothing in response. "Maybe?"

She was shivering. Something raw and primal urged him to pull her into his arms. Warm her. Console her. Not particularly professional. Not particularly *normal*.

"It's only a short walk from the clinic. Just above the horse barns."

Her eyebrows drew together. "It's up a flight of stairs?"

"Yes. Two, I think. In the old hayloft. The apartment overlooks the riding ring. Is that a problem for you?"

"Well, it's not a bad problem, but it's not exactly an ideal health and safety situation." That smile of hers hit her face with full wattage. "Seeing as you like things to be on the up and up, I had just assumed my request had been noted and acted on."

"What request?"

"That my housing be on the ground floor or by an elevator. I did tell Dr. Brennan."

"Cody? He——" Alex bit back the near confession. Cody could be as distracted as he himself could be exacting. They'd met at a conference a few years back when both of their lives had imploded. Alex had been a recent widower and Cody's marriage had just ended. It had sounded as though a lot of his marriage hadn't exactly been a barrel of laughs. That's why they'd dreamed up the clinic. The in-house childcare. The built-in routines their families needed now they no longer had wives.

Alex loved routine. He wasn't as sure about Cody. Though they'd been on the island for three years, the poor guy seemed to be doing about as good a job at leaving the past behind in California as Alex was at remembering where he'd left the happy-go-lucky man his wife had fallen in love with.

Maggie washed the air between them with her hands. "Doesn't matter. I'm sure it'll be fine for now."

"You said it was for health and safety reasons. If there's something I should know…"

Maggie features turned serious then brightened again as if she'd just hit on a solution. "Right. Well. This definitely falls into the super-duper embarrassing department, but it looks like Cody might've forgotten to tell you something important about me."

"Which is?"

He didn't do guessing games. And by the change of her expression she clearly didn't reveal things about herself lightly.

Snap.

She gave her arms a brisk rub as if chivvying herself up to tell him. What on earth could be so big a confession that this force of nature would be wary to reveal it to him?

She hitched up her trouser legs and looked down.

"I'm a double amputee."

"Ah." Alex looked down and saw her prosthetics neatly fitted into her trainers. "It looks as though Dr. Brennan did neglect to mention your...situation."

"Yeah. Double below-the-knee amputations when I was thirteen. Ain't bacterial meningitis a bitch?"

For the first time in a long time, Alex's poker face befriended him.

"Yes. I suppose it can be." He looked into Maggie's eyes. Infinitesimal flashes of worry flashed through her chocolate-colored irises as she waited for his response. A total sea change from the fiery woman he'd met on the rocking deck of a grounded ferry.

Everything he'd presumed about her was flipped on its head.

She wasn't overzealous. She was determined.

She wasn't irresponsibly spontaneous. She was resourceful.

Every single thing she did came with a set of calculated risks.

And she took them.

Grit. Stamina. Pride.

Those were the things that had seen her through the challenges that came each and every day. Not foolishness. He knew the traits well. They were all traits required of a soldier on a battlefield.

She hadn't asked for help. Not once. All her energies had been focused on looking after her patients. Just like any other medical professional. Which was clearly how she wanted to be treated.

And just like that his respect for her doubled again.

Not that he was going to tell her. Maggie struck him as the type who'd see compassion as pity and heaven knew he was no stranger to being on the wrong side of the pity stick.

As nonchalantly as he could he said, "It looks as though some alternative arrangements will have to be made."

She pushed out her lower lip and tipped her head back and forth as if this sort of thing happened all the time.

"No problem. In other news. I'm still freezing. Any chance we can get me a blanket or I can find some other way to get up to the apartment? I'm sure a few days there will be fine. It's not like you get massive lightning storms setting places on fire in the dead of winter, do you?" She gave her arms another rub.

Actually...

Before he could tell her there were a bunch of meteorology students holed up in one of their parents' mansions on the far side of the island, hoping for a rare thunder snowstorm, she batted away her own question.

"Don't listen to me. I'm a bit of a babbler. I mean, *sometimes* you should listen to me. Like when I'm talking about patients. But right now? Probably best to ignore just about everything I say. Except about the being cold part."

Alex nodded as things clicked into place at a rate of knots. The slight hitch to her gait on the docks. She'd been fine on the ferry, or so he'd thought, but suddenly the guide ropes made more sense. She had needed them for the extra support if she'd been as bashed about as he had been on the journey back, and, of course, the incident with Salty had had her literally on her knees... Hell. The pain she must be in.

Clearly mistaking his lack of response for uncertainty about her work ethic, Maggie launched into another one of her high-speed monologues. "It won't impede my work in any way. I've got several sets of legs, all made to exacting specification for each patient I work with. If it's hydro, equine, or a long slow walk on the beach, I'm covered." She grinned. "I even have an awesome new pair of snow boots."

Alex pulled a blanket from a nearby storage cupboard, belatedly spurred into action by the sound of her chattering teeth. They both stared at it as he held it aloft, torn between simply handing it to her or snapping it open, wrapping it round her then pulling her to him. Feeling his body heat cross over to her. Letting his warmth become her warmth.

Shards of anger replaced the carnal thoughts. She was a *colleague,* not a love interest. Even if his below-the-belt brain insisted on picturing her in his bed for the night, his actual above-the-shoulders brain did not. The woman clearly brought chaos in her wake.

Some people were just like that.

Hurricane Maggie.

Patients stranded at sea in a winter storm. Salty's broken leg. He didn't need any more drama in his life other than what crossed his desk professionally. He cleared his throat with a sharp cough and handed her the blanket. "No. The apartment is out of the question. I'm sure it won't surprise you to know I take OSHA regulations seriously."

"Yeah, but—"

"Yeah, but nothing."

Maggie actually laughed.

"What?"

"You sounded just like my father when I wanted to go bungee-jumping."

Bungee-jumping? What the—? *Focus.*

"I *am* a father. So perhaps addressing foolish behavior comes naturally. Or maybe you're accustomed to being told off for it?"

Too sharp. Why was he being such an ass?

Maggie thought his response was hilarious.

"Something like that." She let out a low whistle. "Suffice it to say I wouldn't want to be on the wrong end of your cranky stick when the mud-pie recipe went wrong."

She snorted then paled. "Gosh. I'm sorry. I mean, I know you're a widower, so I'm not making any judgements about your parenting skills or anything. Or trying to be personal. Because I hate that. You know, when people try to go all 'I get your misery' so let's tell each other our life stories."

They stared at one another in horror.

"Just a little bit like I'm doing now. At least I'm not over-sharing. Sometimes I can go straight off the barometer on the TMI front. You ever do that? Tell someone too much? No... I'm guessing no. From the look on your face I'm thinking...just about never..."

She looked as mortified as he felt.

Why was he responding to her like a combination of abominable snowman and robot?

Why did he keep staring at her mouth?

No prizes for coming up with an answer for that. She had the fullest mouth he'd ever seen. And not bright red either...more of a...dusty rose color. Extraordinary. All her features were striking—creamy skin, a smattering of freckles that complemented her feisty approach to life, the dark brown eyes that asked a thousand questions all at once—but those lips of hers...especially the upper one. He wondered what it would be like to trace a finger along— No, he didn't. He didn't wonder anything of the sort.

"Alex? Dr. Kirkland? Yoo-hoo! Eyes are up here...just above the nose. Can we just...you know...start over? Pretend the last few hours didn't happen? I'm really looking forward to working here and I'm not entirely sure we've gotten off on the best...er...foot."

A normal person would have laughed, reached out a conciliatory hand and welcomed her to the fold. A normal person would have apologized for reacting so strangely. A normal person wouldn't feel as if his entire emotional vault had been blasted open and exposed parts of him he'd never thought he'd see again.

"No," he said. "I think it would be best if you stayed at my house."

Oh, good grief. The blood really had left his brain.

Maggie clearly thought so, too. Her eyes widened and her hands went up in protest. "Sleeping with the boss? No, thank you."

That surge of blood missing from his brain had clearly shot directly to an area he had been hoping to keep out of this discussion.

He yanked the zipper up on his winter coat, feeling a hell of a lot more like a teenage boy than the founder of a state-of-the-art medical clinic. "Miss Green, may I kindly remind you we run a professional establishment here. This is not spring break in Florida."

What the...? How had his thoughts leapt from housing a colleague to Maggie Green prancing about amidst sunlit waves in a bikini? Not that the idea of seeing her in a bikini was unappealing. Quite the opposite, in fact. Another blast of red-hot desire blasted in below his belt buckle.

She began shifting from foot to foot and he didn't think she was waiting to go to the ladies' room.

"For a night or so," he clarified. "Not for the duration of your contract."

"I'm sure I'd be fine in a hospital bed."

"I'd feel better if I knew you were being properly looked after." See? He had valid reasons. It was smart. Sensible.

Maggie flicked her thumb toward the wards. "I'm pretty sure I saw an entire medical team in there."

"Who have patients to look after."

Why was he was pressing this? Insisting she stay at his house? He had stairs. Only about ten compared to the thirty-odd she'd have to negotiate on the switchback stairwell up to the top of the barn apartment, but...

She was looking at him expectantly. Clearly hoping for a real reason.

C'mon. Why are you doing this?

Because she spelled trouble and he wanted to make sure she stayed out of it?

Maybe. That was definitely a component.

Because she'd unleashed a billion questions in him and he wanted to find out the answers to at least a few of them before she started work here?

He was getting warmer.

She scared and intrigued him in equal measures, but... against all the odds...he liked her.

Bingo!

"So, how about we get you warmed up over at the house?"

Maggie was still looking at him through dubious eyes cast to half-mast.

Why wasn't she answering? It was a nice enough invitation, wasn't it? A night at the boss's house. What more could a woman who'd just risked life and limb to cross to Maple Island want after she'd admitted she was chilled to the bone and wanted nothing more than to crawl into bed on her own?

Her own space, you idiot.

"We have apple pie."

Good grief. That had sounded about as desperate as it got.

It got her attention, though. Brown eyes all doe-wide and blinking with disbelief.

"You made apple pie?"

Even he had to concede this did stretch the realms of believability. "No. It's a Brady Bistro and Bakery special. Tom Brady's wife, Fiona, made it."

"Is that bakery the one with the huge gingerbread houses at Christmas?" Her eyes glittered as she clapped her hands together then quickly drew the blanket back around herself.

"The one and only. Look, you're obviously freezing, so we should sort this out." He held a hand out in the direction of a seating area. "Perhaps you'd like a moment to consider the proposition on your own?"

Why was he speaking like an uptight nineteenth-century British butler?

"No, thank you, Jeeves," she teased.

Something tightened in his chest and the shock of figuring out what it was nearly made him follow through.

He'd almost *laughed*.

Just like "old Alex" would've done. Would have found the ability to see the lighter side of a pretty insane situation. He wasn't entirely sure how he felt about that. Walls and defenses and inscrutable expressions were…protective. Not that he was hiding away from life or anything. He was living life. *Choosing* life. More importantly, he'd built a *quality* life for his son, whose daycare was on site, who could walk to school and bring home an apple pie when his dad remembered to call ahead to the bakery.

Who wouldn't want that for their child when they'd already endured the greatest loss imaginable? Safety. Security. Protection.

Oh, God.

He *was* hiding from life.

The revelation hit him harder than any physical blow ever could.

What the hell was this woman made of? Ordinary flesh and blood she was not.

He'd known her, what? A handful of hours and already he didn't know if he'd rather never lay eyes on her again or…a whole lot of other things he hadn't considered in a while.

Maggie Green was a whole different variety of sugar and spice. But it wasn't just her physical beauty that had him by the throat. It was the aura of strength that virtually glowed around her.

She exuded life. Vibrancy. And everyone else but him seemed immune to it.

Chemistry.

That's what it was. Good old-fashioned chemistry.

The power of it crackled through him like an electric shock. Empowered rather than diminished. A sensation he wasn't sure he'd ever experienced before.

Maggie finally broke the silence fizzing expectantly between them. "Shall I just say yes to make this all seem a bit less weird?"

"I think that would be wise."

Maggie held out one of her hands and watched the big, fat flake settle onto her palm. "Is that snow?"

Alex turned and looked up to the sky.

He had the kind of profile a girl could stare at for days and still find something new.

Solid. Kind.

Not that she'd made him look away from her just so she could stare at him or anything.

Maybe a little?

She dropped her gaze to his shoulders. Broad. Not bulky or anything. A solid line of strength. They hadn't even sagged as much as a millimeter when he'd hoicked up her duffel bags whose weight had thwarted any number of previous would-be gallants. Not that he was being gallant or anything. Or that she had a herd of suitors following in her wake. She'd made sure of that for quite some time, thank you very much.

Her credo for the past three years had been to focus on work and abandon any attempt at having a personal life.

So crushing on her new boss? Totally *verboten.*

She went back to weather talk.

"I thought this wasn't meant to come until tomorrow." She'd have to dig those snow boots out sharpish.

"Looks like everything's coming early this week." He flicked her a quick look, those green eyes of his taking in so much more than her delight at a handful of snowflakes.

Okay. She wasn't entirely sure if he meant that as a good thing or a bad thing.

She held out her hand again and watched another fat flake descend on it. Snow meant a lot of things for her. The beauty of it, of course. But it meant her crutches would probably have to come out to provide a bit of extra balance in case it froze. She never liked showing off all the things she *couldn't* do at a new workplace. She could pull her cane out. She had a really cool one with a jigger of rum hidden in the handle in lieu of a St. Bernard to carry round a little barrel for her. Not that she was an alcoholic or anything. Far from it. She liked control and getting drunk wasn't really the best means of keeping one's grip on reality. She only had the one experience to hold up to the light and suffice it to say she didn't like holding up her darkest days for re-examination all that often.

Alex narrowed his eyes.

She shivered again and this time it wasn't because she was feeling cold.

Damn.

She was going to secretly start calling him X-Ray Eyes. Or Jeeves, as it betrayed less paranoid vulnerability on her part.

"All the more reason to get you inside and warmed up."

Big Bad Wolf?

Was the big bad wolf meant to be sexy?

Maggie tried to scrunch away an image of Alex the Wolf luring her into his lair as the real Alex nodded toward a path leading out from the clinic's picture-perfect wraparound porch. He picked up his pace as the snowfall increased.

Right. Operation Get Warm. Just follow the man and banish the saucy ideas. She pinned her eyes to his back and promptly skidded on a bit of ice. A searing shot of pain obliterated all other thoughts.

Maggie clenched her jaw against the throbbing in her

knees. Now that the adrenaline of getting the children across to the island had passed and, of course, Salty being all trussed up by the island's other cheer bomb of a doctor, Cody Brennan, the pain and cold of the day were beginning to seep well below the surface.

"Maggie, heads up. We're just going to take a left down this path here."

She scanned the paved path bordered by a sprawl of lush lawn and a low hedge of something she imagined would burst into flower come springtime. A cluster of trees blocked any view of his house. Bummer. If she knew exactly how long it was—

Ten-second windows of time.

She could do anything for ten seconds. And then she could do it again. It's how she'd gotten through her own rehab and how she got scores of her own patients through theirs. Step by step. Day by day. Living each day as if it were her first and her last. No regrets.

Well.

There was one, but…it was harder to appreciate the ups in life if there weren't some downs.

She shook her head and looked up when she realized Alex was speaking to her. "It's a short walk. Forty seconds. A minute tops. Hidden behind that copse of trees there."

What the—?

Ah. The penny dropped. He'd seen she was in pain. He was a doctor. He had a *walking lab* in his clinic. He was giving her goals without patronizing her.

He *understood.*

An emotion bomb exploded in her chest so fast and furious she didn't realize she was wiping tears off her cheeks until she blinked away another set. The only blessing was that Alex hadn't seen them. She blamed the fatigue because the last thing she had ever been was a crier.

Ever since she'd lost her legs, her parents had drilled into her that she was neither handicapped nor was she "handicapable", or whatever other positive affirmation phrase was currently in use. They changed so often it was hard to keep up.

To her parents? She was their daughter. To the high school she had just entered? She was plain ol' Maggie Green. No special treatment. No hiding out in a classroom at lunchtime. No giving up the sports or horse riding that she'd loved for just about forever. Nothing. Just an ordinary kid living an ordinary life.

Obstacles weren't roadblocks. They were opportunities to find solutions. Again and again her parents reminded her that the Grand Canyon had begun as an itty-bitty stream. Mt. Rushmore had started with one solitary chink of a chisel. New York City had not been built in a day. Yeah. They'd laid it on thick.

When she'd discovered para-equestrianism? She'd learned about the joy of goals. And with all of the other kids at the specialist camps who had been dealing with a huge array of disabilities, she'd finally begun to feel just like anyone else. Maybe she'd been a little bit more intense. Once she'd really settled into the disability riding circuit she'd spread her wings and become captured by the idea of joining the American Paralympics team and had set herself the goal of becoming a sprinter.

A sponsor had taken interest in her and had bought her her first set of running blades. Then a fashion designer had made her some high heels. Another had hand-sewn her some fabulous riding boots. She'd vowed to make good on the investment each of those people had made in her. But mostly she'd done it to prove to herself that she could.

After she'd won equestrian gold at a national level, she'd then moved on to the international playing field, and all sorts of other opportunities had come out of the woodwork. More running. Gold medals had come there, too. Ways of reinventing herself so that people had thought of her as powerful rather than pitiful.

Being Maggie Green didn't mean dealing with hum-drum teenage problems of acne and the freshman fifteen. With the new legs she had been offered she could change her body in ways no other teen at her school could. Taller. Shorter. Faster. Steadier. Whatever she'd wanted had been within reach. And that was how she'd lived her life.

Until three years ago when she'd met Eric.

She swallowed hard.

That bit of personal history would always be an incredibly bitter pill to swallow. Proof, if she'd needed it, that she was just as mortal as the next girl.

"Here we are."

Without her having even noticed—score one to thinking deep thoughts—they'd arrived in front of a picture-perfect New England farmhouse.

It was absolutely gorgeous. Not pretentious or oversized. Just the right amount of porch and house all kitted out with big old country windows aglow with enough floor lamps to make the place look unbelievably inviting. Funny. She hadn't really imagined Alex living in a place any more cozy than an exam room.

Not that the clinic hadn't given her an indication of the "personal style" he might lean toward.

The Maple Island Clinic was a former colonial mansion lovingly restored to postcard perfection. The interior was an immaculate, up-to-date medical facility. Light. Bright. Beautifully laid out. A piece of living history. She had yet to have a full tour, but wandering through in wet clothes and shivering like a greyhound in a blizzard didn't seem the best of times to suggest having one.

But this house? *His* house?

He might have to tear her from the doorway once they'd found somewhere else for her to stay.

White clapboard. Wraparound porch. *Ramps.* She wasn't sure why they were there, but she was grateful. Her knees were actually killing her and stairs were a genuine bug-bear at moments like these.

Not that she was going to admit that to Alex.

He put her bags down, opened the already unlocked door, swung her duffel bags inside the entryway and tipped his head toward the stairwell she could see shooting straight up to the broad second floor landing.

He popped his coat onto the row of cast-iron hooks by the door and said, "Let's get you in the shower."

Maggie flushed from her décolletage straight up to her hairline.

"What? No. I'm good. I can do that on my own. Pretty seasoned in that department."

"I meant alone," he intoned dryly.

"Ah. Yes. Of course, Doctor."

She grinned, stepped across the threshold, her foot snagging on the corner of her blanket as she did so and upsetting her already tenuous balance to go flying. Straight into Dr. Alex Kirkland's arms.

CHAPTER FIVE

ALEX DIDN'T EVEN stop to think.

He scooped Maggie up and into his arms and carried her straight up the stairs. She was freezing, exhausted and didn't need another hurdle to leap. Or, in this case, a set of stairs to climb.

"Set me down! I'm not some damsel in distress."

He kicked open the bathroom door.

"Are those waterproof?" He nodded at her prosthetics.

"Up to ten feet," she confirmed through chattering teeth.

"Right." He scanned the room for a minute, surprised at how light she felt in his arms. A rod of steel disguised as a butterfly.

He stared at the bath for a minute then dismissed it. It would take too long to fill. The walk-in shower would have to do.

"Hey! Wait a minute. I normally have a chair for showering."

He unceremoniously deposited her on the toilet seat.

"What the—? I'm not just some rag doll you can fling around, bud."

Bud? Since when he had he gone from *Doctor* to *bud*?

Since you scooped her up like Tarzan and dumped her on the toilet seat, you idiot.

"If I wasn't a guest in your house, I'd—"

He turned to face her, their eyes clashing like two rivals taking that all-important final turn at a duel. She was a turbocharged combination of fury and barely contained tolerance.

"Yes? What would you do if you weren't my guest?"

"I'd—I'd at least make sure there was a huge pile of fluffy towels before putting me in that thing."

He felt another twist in his chest, that rare thump straight in the solar plexus telling him what he really wanted to do was laugh. But he was still too jacked up on adrenaline to go there.

"Don't move."

She rolled her eyes. As if, the expression said. Blue lips, knees literally knocking together. It wasn't like they were going to start a farcical chase scene round the smattering of bedrooms he had upstairs.

He "drove" his wheelie chair from his office into the bathroom.

"Yeah. No. Uh-uh. That's not going to happen." Maggie spun her index finger alongside her head.

"What? You don't like the wheels?"

"Er...that and...actually...maybe the wheels would be handy."

She didn't look entirely sure. He'd rip them off if necessary.

He reached into the shower and cranked the controls onto full blast. "Rainforest or handset?"

"Warm."

Right. Of course. He was wasting time.

He pulled the chair into the tiled shower, scooped Maggie up again, minus the blanket, placed her onto the cushioned seat, then wheeled her directly under the warm flow of water after tilting it slightly so she didn't feel as though he'd stuck her under a waterfall. One of the many pluses of life on Maple Island? Excellent water pressure.

See? Still practical. At least there was one thing he could

rely on when the rest of his senses were on some maniacal drive to overrule him and exist again.

"Temperature okay?"

"Great."

"There's body-wash, shampoo, whatever you need. Towels next door, which, of course, I will get. Would you like a hand with your prosthetics?"

"Alex?"

"Yup?" He stared directly into her eyes, surprised to see them bright with hints of amusement.

"Any chance you're going to get out or were you just going to strip off with me and call it a date?"

The laughter that had trickled into her throat turned into full-on giggles.

He looked down at his clothes. Completely drenched. Of course they were. He was standing in a shower. An urge to start peeling his clothes off stripper style seized him when the bump on her forehead caught his attention again. She saw him notice it and put her hand up.

He grabbed it before she reached the bump, and when their hands touched?

Heat explosion.

He dropped her hand as if he'd grabbed a burning coal. She pressed her own to her forehead with a sharp inhalation.

Damn. Way to handle simple body contact, Alex.

She had thrown him well off course. Sure, she was cold. She was hurt. But since when did he carry women across the threshold of his home, up the stairs and stand in the shower with them as if it were completely normal?

Did she have a magic wand tucked away somewhere in that winter wear of hers?

If she did, was the magic benevolent or from somewhere entirely more fiery and unpredictable? A flash of electricity crackled through his entire body. It was as if she'd flicked on a long-dormant switch and pushed the power demand up to its highest level. Turned the volume straight up to eleven.

He stared at her as the water cascaded down her face, little droplets sliding along each feature, each freckle, those full lips of hers. Electricity and warm running water was a pretty lethal combination if the hammering in his chest was anything to go by.

You are a doctor. She is hurt. Behave like a normal human. Not a dormant creature suddenly brought back to life after a long, interminable freeze.

He knelt before her and sat back on his heels, his voice dropping to somewhere deep in his chest he hadn't accessed before.

"Let me have a look. When did this happen?"

"I told you." Her voice was barely above a whisper as her eyes remained locked with his. "The ambulance ride over. It's been this way all day."

Had it? Of course it had. He was being an idiot. A cursory glance said it wouldn't need stitches, it was just an abrasion, but...even so...a bandage wouldn't go amiss.

Was he only noticing it now because he was finally noticing *her*? The actual Maggie Green rather than a recent hire who'd arrived in a tornado of chaos?

Maybe the electricity that had been zapping between the pair of them all day hadn't been exasperation after all, or two diametrically opposite people actively repelling each other.

It was attraction. Plain and simple. Didn't even need to be a neurosurgeon to figure that one out and so here he was. A neurosurgeon soaked to the bone in his own shower, kneeling in front of a flame-haired beauty whose dark eyes were burning holes straight through to his soul.

They stared at each other in silence. The water cascading down their heads, their faces...her neck...the dips and curves that led to her breasts...the flat length of her belly. Her chest rose and fell with short, quick breaths as he drank her in.

And then she blinked.

He didn't blame her. The moment was intense. Too intense. If anyone had told him a year ago—hell, two hours ago—that he was going to be kneeling at the feet of his new physio as if she were Aphrodite herself he would've... Well, he wouldn't have laughed. That's for sure.

"To be honest," Maggie confessed, "it's my knees that got more of a bashing than my head."

He forced himself to drop his gaze to her knees. She was still wearing trousers and, thanks to the warm water pouring over them, they were sticking to her like latex.

"Do these come off any way other than the usual way?"

"'Fraid not."

"I think we should take them off and—"

"Um, no, sir. I think you'll find the 'we' in this whole scenario is more like *you'd* better get your butt out of here and find *me* some towels. I'll sort out my own business, thank you very much."

She spoke with absolute confidence. Her eyes told another story.

She didn't want him to see her legs.

Fair enough.

No! Not fair enough. He was a doctor and for all intents and purposes, right now she was under his care and her knees might need patching up.

"Sorry. My roof, my rules."

She arced an astonished eyebrow at him. "Excuse me?"

He pressed himself up so that he was no longer sitting back on his heels but kneeling so that they were eye to eye.

"I am a doctor. I am your boss. You are my responsibility. You are safe with me."

Together they processed what he'd said.

You are my responsibility. You are safe with me.

Big words from a man who had promised the same to a little boy with a dead mother.

She hadn't followed the orders that would have saved her life. She'd had responsibilities, a son, *and still she hadn't followed orders.*

Maggie must've seen his thoughts drift. His indecision. She gave another one of those flippant shrugs of hers, flicking her tightly corkscrewing curls behind her shoulders.

"Yeah. I'm pretty clear about who's who and what the lie of the land is, *Dr.* Kirkland. Doesn't mean I can't get my own clothes off."

"I think I should have a look at your knees. We want our staff to be staff, not patients."

She cocked her head to the side, maintaining such a high level of intensity in her gaze he felt as though they were physically connected.

"Fine. As long as you don't look."

It took him a few seconds to realize she was taking off her clothes.

Practical Alex would've gotten out of the shower and found a plastic laundry basket to put everything in and run down to the dryer. Responsible Alex would have looked away.

He didn't let his gaze dip. That would betray the trust she was investing in him, if that's what she was doing. Perhaps it was a dare. A test.

It definitely *felt* like a test and something told him Maggie Green didn't tolerate people who couldn't cross the finish line when it came to keeping their word.

Their eyes were caught in a magnetic hold. He forced the breath in his chest to stay even. Steady. Even though his pulse was pounding away in his brain, continuing to send the bulk of his blood flow into regions that weren't entirely useful. At least, not in this scenario.

From the movement of her body he could see she was hitching herself up on one hip, then the other, pulling her trousers off what he imagined would be the smooth curves of her derriere and down along her hips, then her thighs. He ached to look. But betraying her trust was not an option. He wanted her to know he was honorable. That she could count on him. Even if it meant suppressing the millions of electric currents his body was begging him to find a use for.

Eyes still steadily hooked on his, Maggie pulled one of her knees up, the toe of her running shoe grazing along the length of his chest as she pulled it up to the chair. His fault, not hers. He should've moved back. But he couldn't move. Not even when it had felt as though she'd dragged a hot poker along his chest.

He heard her shoe fall to the floor with a little splash, then she repeated the whole thing again. The toe of her second shoe seared along the length of his chest, her eyes unblinking as she removed and dropped it to the tiled surface of the shower floor. The sound of saturated fabric shifting around her ankles and a little flick of her legs told him her trousers were now off. She leant toward him and they both tipped their heads forward as she took hold of the soaked material and pulled it onto her lap.

Their heads touched, lightly. They both looked up and at each other. He could feel her breath on his lips. He wanted to cup her face in his hands and kiss her. And not just any old kiss. An urgent, hungry, satiating kiss. Something that would answer all of the questions he'd had from the moment he'd laid eyes on her. Something that would tell him if all of this was a hallucination or very, very real.

"Ready, Doc?"

He nodded, not entirely sure what he was saying he was ready for.

Maggie sat back in the chair and detached her prosthetic, their eyes still locked on each other's. He was going to kiss her. Resistance seemed...ridiculous. Why wait for something he'd never known he wanted?

So he did.

He didn't hover nervously. Offer tentative butterfly kisses. No. His mouth crashed down on hers as if he'd been waiting for this moment his entire life.

From the moment his mouth touched hers, he knew that lightning could strike twice. That there was more than one woman he'd been meant to kiss. To hold. To cup her face between his hands. To taste as the water poured over the pair of them, erasing time, history, anything and everything that up until this moment would've kept them apart.

It wasn't a one-sided kiss. Not by a long shot. Maggie's entire body was arching up and toward him. She'd woven her fingers through his hair and was sliding her other hand along his stubble as their kisses gained in intensity.

Just as he was about to slip his hands onto her waist and pull her even closer to him, the bathroom door abruptly slammed open.

Alex pulled himself away from Maggie and turned just in time to see his son walk through the door.

Jake. His little boy. A mop of sandy blond hair, just like his. Brown eyes like his mother's. As if he'd ever forget who had brought this child into the world. His serious, intense, loving son who'd gone through all but a single year of his life without his mother.

"Hey, Dad." Jake's eyebrows tugged together as he took in the scene then noticed that Maggie was holding one of her legs in her hand. His eyes widened further than Alex had ever seen them.

"Oh...." His eyebrows rose up to his hairline. *"Cool...."*

Maggie would've happily stayed in "her" bedroom for the rest of the night. After Alex had all but bolted out of the shower, he'd thrown the promised stack of fluffy towels into the room then left her to get on with things on her own. She'd taken her time luxuriating in the warm flow of water but she wasn't cold anymore. Not by a long shot.

The moment their lips had touched, wildfire had scorched through her body and left nothing but hot embers in its wake.

In reality, she should've turned the water temperature down to cold the moment he'd left. No one—and by no one she actually meant not a single solitary human—had ever made her feel so damn sexy so damn fast.

Her fingers had still been shaking when she'd given her knees some long overdue TLC. They were sore all right, but nothing too major. When she'd finally gotten out of the shower and wrapped her body and hair in a pair of those thick cotton towels, she'd seen that Alex had slipped a note under the door saying he'd retrieved a wheelchair from the clinic for her and some spare crutches if she didn't want to put her prosthetics back on that night.

As much as it had pained her to admit it, for tonight her reserves of stoicism were depleted. Alex had been right to invite her across to his house. And kind. There was something extra comforting about being in a home rather than bunking in the hospital, which, as lovely as it was, would've been a bit too much like…well…staying in a hospital.

She'd wheeled along behind him in the low, sling-backed wheelchair—both of them pretending they had barely met let alone had a Class-A make-out session in the shower. When she'd seen past the bedroom door he'd swung open for her she'd sighed with delight. A big old low-riding sleigh bed she wouldn't have to worry about mountain climbing in and out of. She could literally fall out of bed and not risk further injury. There was a thick comforter covered by a cleverly designed patchwork quilt that looked as though someone's grandmother had sewn it long ago. Alex's maybe? His wife's?

Everything about the softly lit room was so sumptuous and inviting it all but screamed for her to come in and sleep. Sleep away all of her worries and start over tomor-

row, but Alex had stiffly insisted she join them for a din-
ner of lasagna, garlic bread and salad. And, of course, the
apple pie. When Jake had peeked out from behind his father's back, a blue satin cape tied round his shoulders, and
put his hands together in a praying position she'd relented.

Alex had offered to carry her down, sensing that putting her prosthetics on again might be an ask too far. She'd
laughed off his suggestion and made some crack about not
wanting to do his back in.

In truth? She didn't want to be that close to nestling
her nose and lips up against that neck of his. That special
warm spot she now knew smelt of juniper and sea air. Not
that she'd been breathing him in like a life-affirming es-
sential oil in the shower or anything, but... Oh, all right.
She had been. He actually smelled of dedication, if such
a thing was possible. Fidelity. And something unique to
him. Eau d'Alex.

Whatever it was, if she'd been a teenager she would've
bought a bottle of it and put a few drops on her pillow every
night in the hope of some less-than-pure dreams.

She also knew that whatever it was would make her
want to kiss him again.

Which was why when her *new boss* had offered to carry
her down the stairs a second time, she'd given him a solid
no.

Jake had suggested she slide down the wooden banister,
even though his dad wouldn't let him do it. Maybe, Jake
had said with a wistful look in his eyes, he'd let her. Alex
had given his son a glare. There had been love in it. But
definitely a glare.

Risking a glare of her own, she'd said she'd like to try
something she hadn't done in ages. Bump down the stairs
on a pillow. Before she'd barely finished her sentence Jake
had rushed off and returned with two pillows covered in
a superhero motif.

Alex had compressed his lips then said, "If you're going

to do it, you may as well do it in comfort. And *safety*."
He ducked into a room—his office, she presumed—and
emerged with two extra-thick sofa cushions and two helmets, one hockey and one bicycle.

"Do you always keep helmets in your office?"

"Yes," he'd replied. "Stops me from having a head injury when I'm doing the clinic's accounts. Spreadsheets
aren't my forte."

One by one she and Jake had bumped their way down
the broad wooden staircase. He'd done a victory dance
when they'd landed then he'd offered to pull her to the
kitchen. Like a carriage horse. She wasn't sure of it, but
after she'd pulled her helmet off and shaken her hair out,
she was pretty certain when she'd looked up and seen Alex
on the top landing, he'd been smiling.

Half an hour into their shared supper, she was really
pleased she'd made the effort.

All the tension that had been snapping and popping between Alex and her had smoothed into something more...
fun. Especially as Alex seemed to have handed any and
all conversational reins over to Jake.

"Daddy told me that before you came here you were in
the Paralympics?"

Oh? *Daddy must've visited the internet while she'd been
in the shower.*

"That's right. Equestrian and running."

"Did you win medals?"

"Sure did!" She feigned an in-chair running move and
crooned, "Lean, mean Maggie Green gets *gold*!"

She made fake crowd cheering noises and Jake joined
in. She didn't dare look at Alex. She didn't want him to
think she was bragging. It was just fun to bring a smile
to Jake's face. He was so *earnest*. It felt like being inter-
viewed for *The Times*.

"Were you born like that?"

"Jake!" Alex scrubbed his hand across his face and sent an apologetic grimace through his fingers.

She waved it off. Kids' questions were open. Honest. It was good old-fashioned curiosity and nothing more.

"I got sick when I was thirteen with something called bacterial meningitis and my lower legs had to be amputated."

His mouth dropped open. "You mean they sawed them off?" He looked equal parts horrified and delighted.

"Jake!" Alex half rose in his chair in warning.

Maggie laughed and indicated for him to sit back down again. "Honestly, it's fine. And, yup, that's pretty much what happened." No point in glossing over it. Kids weren't judgmental. They just thought it was cool she'd been sawn up.

She looked down at her knees, grateful her parents had made the call when they had. If they'd waited any longer... well, life as an above-the-knee amputee was perfectly acceptable, but she wouldn't have been able to do a lot of the things she could if they had waited.

"My parents encouraged me to get back to my horse riding and when I saw some of the Paralympians riding, I was so excited. And as for running..." she gave them both a *How could I not want some of those?* grin "...I had to get me some of those blades, right?"

Jake popped his chin into his cupped hand and stared at her for a moment. Alex rose and fetched the apple pie from the counter.

"Since you can change your legs, does that make you like a superhero?"

Jake was, she saw, completely serious.

So she took the question seriously. Just as she hoped all of her patients took her seriously when she told them at the beginning of whatever program they were pursuing that all of the sweat and tears would be worth it. That no one could ever tell them what they could and couldn't do as long as they put in the work. That they would be masters of their own destinies.

Which, now that she thought about, did make her a bit of a superhero.

"Yes. In some ways it does. But remember, all superheroes also have their kryptonite."

Jake nodded somberly. She'd known him for less than an hour and already it was pretty easy to see the apple hadn't fallen far from the tree. Serious, like his father. Considered. Considerate. It was like meeting a mini-Alex minus the heated looks and the big broad shoulders.

Okay. There were actually quite a few differences, but she really liked this kid. And if Alex had raised him pretty much on his own, it spoke highly of both of them.

She swallowed down a lump of emotion that lodged itself in her throat as she thought of Jake growing up with a father dealing with one of life's most unimaginable griefs. The loss of a loved one.

Her own parents had been her bedrock when she'd become ill. They were gone now and she felt their absence every day, but she also knew their lives together had been rich and full. She'd appeared as a welcome surprise when her mother had been in her late forties and her father in his late fifties. Her father had been a professor of poetry and her mother had taught children how to ride horses at their small farm just outside the city. They had loved life. Found it beautiful, in fact. And had taught her to do the same. There was, after all, only one chance to be yourself. So, they'd reasoned, you may as well live it to the fullest.

The emotion she thought she'd swallowed did a U-turn and returned as a sting of tears.

Twice in one day. What the heck was in the water on this island? High-density emotion particles?

She ignored the inquisitive look Alex sent her when she did a weird throat-clearing thing and focused on Jake. He still had his chin propped in his little hand and was staring at her, maybe trying to see if she'd been hiding any other superpowers.

"Any more questions?"

"When you and Dad were in the shower, did I interrupt you kissing?"

Alex choked on his garlic bread and Maggie did a strangled version of her *as if* laugh.

"No!" they both said in unison. And then, "We weren't kissing!"

"Yes, you were." Jake looked confused. "Or, at least, that's what it looked like to me."

There was a note of hope in his voice that pierced straight through to Maggie's heart.

It must be hard, being the kid without a mom.

She got it. For a short while she'd been like that with legs. *"But, Mom! Everybody else has them!"* Her mother had swiftly reminded her that everyone else did not have the ability to pick and choose as she did. That had made short work of that argument. She supposed it didn't work that way with mothers.

And it didn't always work that way with legs.

Alex's quick glance in her direction hit her with pinpoint accuracy. The idea of his son seeing them kissing was clearly absolutely appalling to him. After scrubbing a *Don't be ridiculous, son* hand through Jake's hair, he looked back at her, lingering this time. Oh...wait a minute. It wasn't revulsion. That was her own paranoia at work. It was being *caught* that had him looking so horrified.

Did it happen like this? Lust at first sight? It couldn't be anything more than that. At least on his side. He'd not even known who she was when he'd woken up this morning.

What she felt wasn't anything more than a grown-up's version of a schoolgirl crush. It couldn't—*wouldn't*—be anything more. Not after what she'd been through. And certainly not with her boss.

Jake stared at the two of them for a moment, shrugged

and moved on, mercifully unable to sense the forty zillion kilowatts of discomfort that were now zinging through the air.

"So, what's your kryptonite, then?" he asked after finishing his milk at his father's request.

Alex's eyes zapped to his son. "That's a bit personal, Jake."

"No, no. It's all right." She liked this sort of straightforward talk. At least from little kids. Besides, she wasn't going to tell him what it really was. She had a stock answer that seemed to satisfy most people. Stopped any follow-up questions. "Having to ask people for help."

It was kind of true. She never liked it, even though she knew people with two legs, two arms and a head screwed on straight asked for help, too. But she wasn't going to tell a little boy that she'd actually stared her kryptonite in the face earlier that evening when his father's lips had been close enough for her to kiss. And she'd fallen at the first hurdle.

Making out with her boss could not be a part of her time here on the island. Intimacy was off the cards. Eric had made sure of that in one swift, nasty strike. Nothing physical. Ever again. That had been the deal.

How about that for ripping a credo to shreds.

Alex shot her a funny look. One that made her think kissing each other might not be on the menu again anyway.

Maybe she could tape her credo back together.

"Should we have pie now?" Jake beamed at her. "I like mine with ice cream."

I like mine with green-eyed doctors in a picture-perfect country kitchen.

"Sounds amazing." She nodded, pleased to catch the slight twitch of a smile tweak at the corners of Alex's mouth. Something about bringing a smile to that man's lips felt rewarding.

"So, tell me, Jake. What's life like here on Maple Island?"

He shot a look at his father and Alex nodded that he could go ahead, say what he liked. She smiled.

Alex was a big old ball of mystery wrapped up in a very male package. When they'd first met she'd thought, *Uh-oh, here we go. Another uptight, regulations first, reality later, non-emotive, surgical type.* But those types didn't sweep girls off their feet, float them up the stairs and put their favorite work chair in the shower and help them undress.

Well.

Watch her undress?

No, *help.*

Definitely help. That's what he'd been trying to do.

Either way, it had been just about the most erotic thing that had happened to her in years.

From the heated look that had been in his eyes and the smoking-hot kisses he'd laid on her lips, she was guessing Alex was in the same camp.

As he handed her a generous triangle of cinnamon-laden pie, the current look in Alex's eyes was almost as intense as it had been in the shower. Telling her she was safe whilst teasing her to take a risk. Reach out and tug not just his shirt collar but at the tight fabric holding the complex layers of his personality together.

"...ride a horse, but Dad won't let me."

"What? Beg pardon? I was in a rapture over this pie," Maggie lied, to cover up the fact she'd actually been daydreaming about teasing apart the layers of his father's hidden depths. And maybe his shirt buttons too.

"Now, that's not strictly true," Alex cut in, a small bite to his otherwise gentle admonition. "I only wanted you to wait until there was someone running the stables who I thought might be more appropriate for you to learn to ride with."

"But Randy worked in the rodeo!" Jake held out his hands as if that clearly made Randy the best possible choice.

"Not to brag or anything, but I think we've established

that I know my way around a horse." She blew on the tips of her fingers and shook them.

"Like a cowgirl?" Jake asked.

"A bit." She was just about to tell him about the handstands and other tricks she could do but caught a warning glance from Alex. "I used to ride dressage competitively."

"What's that? Putting clothes on the horse?" Jake's confused expression was so freaking cute she had to sit on her hands to stop herself from reaching out and ruffling his hair.

Not her son.

Not hers to become besties with in front of the boss after an unexpected kissing session.

"Let me put it this way, compared to barrel racing or some of the other things your friend Randy did, dressage is about as pernickety and exacting as you can get."

"It doesn't sound as fun as barrel racing." Jake's shoulders sagged.

"It sounds safer," Alex commented.

Maggie made a *that's one way to look at it* noise. "My mom thought it was a good way to teach me how to use a different kind of strength to get what I wanted out of a horse."

Jake screwed up his face, confused. Alex leaned in.

Oh, jinks. They were expecting something wise and insightful.

"Honest truth?" She crossed her heart and looked Jake straight in the eye. "My parents thought I could do with dropping my ego. Using common sense instead of frustration to get what I wanted. Horses don't respond well to pent-up teenage angst. They go in for teamwork."

Alex leant back in his chair as if he'd just understood something fundamental about her. She hoped he did. That she wasn't all bells and whistles. She did this work because she cared. She truly cared about her patients and not just their physical welfare but the emotional foundation that they would need to see them through the many hurdles they had to confront as they healed.

"Is that why you came to Maple Island? To work with my daddy's team?"

She swallowed against the real reason and nodded. "Sure is."

"Why would you want to be here, though, when you could be in the Paralympics?"

She laughed. "As much as I would like to have done it forever, I thought it'd be a good idea to pay back some of the kindness I received when I was in training."

Jake gasped. "You gave away your medals?"

"No." She hadn't looked at them in a while, though. After Eric, she hadn't felt as proud of her accomplishments as she once had. "I thought if I became a physiotherapist I could help my patients with a lot of the things I learned over the years." Grit. Determination. That feeling of over-coming adversity was the best in the world as long as you made sure you picked wisely in the romance department.

Her eyes kept flicking across to Alex, who was thought-fully scrubbing his jaw as his son continued to pepper her with questions. What was dressage? Were the Paralympics every year or like the Olympics? Could she jump a horse from here to Boston? Where were her medals? Why didn't she wear them like necklaces? If he had medals he would wear them every day.

Her brain was registering the questions, but her body was tingling with a whole other set of sensations. Her fin-gertips wished they were his…feeling his stubble. The stip-pled silkiness of it against her fingers. The softness of his lips. The heat.

Alex barely looked at her as he pushed around the scant remains of pie left on his plate. A feigned disinterest or actually not interested?

Maybe the whole shower incident had been a freak oc-currence and that's why he was letting his son do the interrogating for him. He was taking a clear step back from the obvious connection they'd shared.

Fair enough.

She tore her eyes away and focused on answering all of Jake's questions.

Tomorrow Alex wouldn't just be her host, he would be her boss.

CHAPTER SIX

"THEY TOLD ME I'd find you here!"

Maggie knocked on the doorframe again when Salty didn't turn to meet her smile. She waited, her thoughts drifting to that tingling feeling bubbling in her belly when she heard Alex's lovely warm voice as he exchanged patient notes with another doctor.

She was excited to see patients and a little bit scared at how much her body went all giggly schoolgirl when she was around Alex.

She thought back to last night's conversation.

"Are you sure you've had enough ice cream?" Jake had finished off his two scoops lickety-split and made to dish more out to them.

"Two scoops is perfect," she and Alex had said in tandem. Then stared at one another while Jake had laughed and pointed at them.

She'd stretched and yawned, her top riding up as she'd done so, and she'd caught Alex staring at that little triangle of flesh right where her waistline dipped and swooped toward her hip. "Guess it's time to get on up to bed," she'd murmured.

She'd said it to make him blush. And it had worked.

Then she'd felt like an idiot because what was the rule? No flirting. If she didn't flirt, there was no danger of romance and with no danger of romance. She could carry on living with her pride intact.

It hadn't stopped her insides from swirling around like a happy snow globe when Alex had picked her up to go upstairs then paused, turned toward the sofa, dithering about whether or not to make up a bed there "just in case."

"Safety first," he'd said, as seriously as a dentist warned a child who loved cookies to steer clear of desserts.

She'd finally exclaimed she was so tired that if he didn't let her sleep in the bed he'd already shown her she would teach Jake how to wolf whistle. That'd shut him up. And given her time to take just one more surreptitious inhalation of his lovely man scent right there at the crook of his neck. *Mmm....*

"What're you smiling at, girlie?"

Salty's scratchy voice wiped the smile off her face. Today was a work day. Not a day to go around with your head in the clouds remembering the sexy aroma of your boss.

"Ah!" She walked into his room, rubbing her hands together with a renewed sense of purpose. "You *are* alive."

"Might as well be dead for all the use I am in this here contraption." He began fiddling with the sling that was elevating his leg.

"Uh-uh. No, you don't. That leg is up for a reason."

"Don't need more blood in my head than I do in my toes, do I? Otherwise God woulda designed me different."

"Good point. But I'm pretty sure the doctor is keeping your leg elevated to aid in the healing process and it sounds like you would prefer that to be as speedy as possible."

Salty shifted a bit in his bed and gave her a long cold stare. "If by *speedy* you're talking about the six long weeks the doc said I'd be in for after he'd examined me, I think you might be wise to invest in a dictionary. The word means something different than what you seem to think it does, young lady." He harrumphed and turned away again,

his gaze trailing out to the sea view he'd been thought-
fully given.

"Ah! Miss Green. There you are."

Alex came striding into the room all businesslike and
official. She'd watched him morph from dad to doctor over
the breakfast table. She smiled at his officiousness. He almost belonged in another era. One with carriages and foot-
men and...sexy shirtless men walking out of lakes with
nothing but desire in their eyes.

"Miss Green?"

"Yes!" She gave him a quick salute. "Reporting for duty,
sir!"

He gave her a dry look. "I left the military some time
ago, Miss Green, and, as I'm sure you'll recall, we go for
a slightly *gentler* approach around here at the Maple Island Clinic."

"Sir, yes, sir!"

Astonishingly, Salty laughed.

Maggie winced an apologetic look at Alex and flicked
her thumb toward Salty. "Sorry. I just wanted to make sure
he could still do that."

"Yes." His green eyes narrowed then blinked. His expression was virtually impossible to read. "You and mirth
seem to be good friends."

She gave him a simple nod. It was what had kept her
head above water these last three years so she wasn't going
to apologize for it.

"Shall we take that tour you promised?" She tipped
her head toward Salty and said in a stage voice, "I'll come
back and see the hero of the seven seas a bit later. Check
on his progress."

A cantankerous bark of irritation followed her comment but she didn't take it personally. Rarely did when
it came to patients. Their response to their own pain was
wholly personal. Nothing to do with her. And then she
winked at Alex.

Why did she keep winking at him?

Mercifully, Alex ignored it.

"You've obviously made yourself familiar with the patients' rooms."

She nearly cracked a joke. Something lame about enjoying having a good snoop behind her employer's back, but reconsidered. She genuinely wanted Alex to know she was good at her job. Minus the jokes. Minus the bravura. The occasional pain.

So she kept her lips pressed together and followed Alex as he gave her an extraordinarily detailed tour of the clinic—including all the fire exits and extinguisher points.

She couldn't help but smile. She would've put money on the fact this fastidious approach to safety—so meticulous it meant no one else had to even think about it—was his way of coping with loss.

She'd chosen another path.

After realizing just how much physio she'd need for the rest of her own life, she'd decided she wanted to know how to do it for herself. One more step in the "take charge of her own destiny" remit her parents had said was all hers for the taking. There had been one point after the debacle with Eric when she'd thought about abandoning people altogether and going down the line of working solely with animals, but her mother, who at this point hadn't been long for the world, had asked her if she was making the decision based on fear or on passion.

It had been fear. Fear of seeing herself in all the patients going through the worst times of their lives. Her mother had gently reminded her that she was, in fact, the best person for those patients to see. To work with. To see what they could become if they set aside their own fears. It had been one of the last conversations she'd had with her mother and the most profound. She'd thought she'd finally conquered all her fears.

Right up until she'd received that text from Eric a couple of days ago.

Hey, beautiful. Guess who's back in Bean Town? Fancy a friendly beer?

Yeah, right. As much as she'd want to be locked in a cage with a ravenous silver-backed gorilla. Actually…she'd choose the gorilla over a "friendly beer" with Eric. There wasn't a solitary cell in his body she thought was capable of true friendship. Which was why she was at the clinic days before she was due to actually start, following Alex Kirkland around like an eager puppy and pretending she didn't want to reach out and accidentally on purpose graze her hand along his unsurprisingly sexy posterior. Or kiss him. Or do both at the same time.

"Have you seen the twins today?"

Alex gave her a quick glance that told her all she needed to know. Of course he had. Dr. Protocol was also Dr. Efficiency from the looks of things. Fair enough. It *was* his clinic.

"How many patients are actually here? Bit of a shame to have to be in the hospital over the holidays."

"It's a bit of a shame to have to be in the hospital at any time." He tipped his head down, those evergreen eyes of his peering at her in a way that would've been better suited to an over the thick-rimmed eyeglasses look. Or a monocle.

Touché, Jeeves.

But also a little bit unnecessary. It wasn't like she of all people didn't know that. Then again, she had made it pretty clear she didn't want special treatment from him.

She gave him a quick nod of acknowledgement then continued on their tour. Work Alex was definitely less accessible than the man at home with his son. Or the Alex who'd shared her shower. And straight away another whoosh of warm sparkles swirled around her stomach and lazily floated down to that sensitive triangle below her belly button as if they had all the time in the world to day-dream about being in a wet and half-naked clinch with her boss.

Stop thinking about what happened in the shower!

She caught up to him and put on her best professional face. "How soon do you think it'll be before I work with them? The twins."

He took in a quick breath. "Oh, I would say fairly sharp-ish."

"What? Right now?"

"Perhaps not this precise instant, given that you are not yet officially an employee," he bit back, stopped himself, then began again. "Forgive me. I didn't get much sleep last night."

"I slept like a baby."

His eyes slid over to meet hers. "I'm pleased to hear it."

He didn't look very pleased and it suddenly struck her that she might be the reason he hadn't slept particularly well. And kaboom! There went the internal electricity, making a mess of her heart rate.

Work. Work talk fixes everything.

"Maybe I could pop in and see them this afternoon. Do a bit of massage." Her fingers flexed involuntarily. She glared at them, then snuck a peek at Alex, whose shoul-ders looked as though they could do with a massage as well. *Urgh! No. Not massage!* "Maybe a bit of TENS?"

Alex gave her a peculiar look then nodded. "Perhaps." He gave that sexy jaw of his a tell-tale scrub, indicating he was thinking, his fingertips drumming along his mouth as he pondered.

What? To fire her? Tell her that her suggestions were terrible?

"As you've arrived early, we can tweak your contract so that you're covered on the insurance front, but I'd quite like you to work alongside me for the week if you don't mind." He held up a hand before she could protest. "I have my methods and you have yours. I'd like to make sure they…" He paused again.

Lordy. The tension was killing her. What? What?

That their methods of work were fluid? Gave them enough time to kiss in between patients? Would give him a reason to rip up the contract and send her back to Boston to face her demons? *What? Speak!*

"I'd like to make sure our methods are on the same page."

Okay. Phew. Same page was something she could work with.

He looked toward Salty's room, "The electric nerve stimulation could help ease any discomfort the twins are having. We've also found ice packs can be useful in short bursts."

"So, is that a long-winded yes?"

"There's still paperwork to be done. You're not technically on staff yet, Maggie."

"I like to make a difference from the moment I arrive."

His eyebrows rose. "Oh. You've done that all right."

Maggie tore her eyes away from his and focused on the long walkway they had just turned onto. It was glassed in so she could see the whole of the central courtyard and sprawl of a snow-blanketed lawn that curved down toward the sea. She felt about as transparent as the walkway.

Kissing her boss a handful of hours after meeting him was sort of a no-brainer in the "recommended things not to do" department.

He started it!

You didn't stop it.

No doubt about it. Alex Kirkland tore down her finely crafted protection system—jokes, goofy faces, zany behavior. Anything to cover up the vulnerability she'd felt ever since Eric had planted that vile earworm straight into her soul.

With you out of pity. Pity. Pity. Pity.

She gave her head a sharp shake and tried to scrub her hands through her untamable hair, only to succeed in making it look more wild than it had before. Alex was giving her a funny look so she fell back on a reliable topic. The weather. Everyone loved a good weather chat. "Looks like it'll be time to make snowmen soon." She smiled at the wintry scene, which reminded her of the farm she'd grew up on. "The snow makes everything look so pure, doesn't it?"

She turned to him as his gaze flicked away.

"Not everything."

He wasn't even looking at her, but the comment lassoed straight into her brain and pulled to the fore all the various kissing scenarios she'd run through last night.

He is not asking you to kiss again.

Try telling the rest of your body that, will you?

Her tongue swept across her lips. Her breasts were perking up. That warm swirl of heat he unleashed in her unfurled in her belly like a saucy serpent.

He turned his head and looked straight at her, his green eyes inscrutable.

Oh, jeez. He was reading her mind and didn't approve. He looked so...*stern.* She almost preferred sexy, soaked-in-the-shower Alex to this guy. Almost.

Sexy Alex scared her more. Made her feel things she'd promised herself she'd never feel again. Like the hot ache of desire that had made her breasts go heavy when he'd pulled her to him. Had heated up that private triangle below her belly button in a way no man had before. Seeing the fire in Alex's eyes had sparked a warm, pulsing need deep within her for something she'd vowed never to do again.

Not after Eric.

She changed her pace so that she was walking slightly behind Alex as her memories rushed to the fore. She and Eric had met through friends at Boston Harbor Hospital.

He'd been enthusiastic. Too enthusiastic, she'd thought at the time but had pushed her concerns to the side. He'd made her feel beautiful. Interesting. Valued. She'd been wary to steam ahead with the physical side of things. Something about the way he'd kept saying the fact she was an amputee was "super-cool" had niggled at her. She hadn't figured out exactly why until one day when kissing hadn't been enough and they'd decided to take things further. Tops had been unbuttoned. Her skirt had been unzipped and discarded. She'd instinctively started to take off her legs. She had in previous relationships, so...no big deal, right?

His face had told her all she'd needed to know. But he'd kept on talking.

"Soz, Maggie," Eric had said. "I just can't do it."

She'd been stupid enough to ask, "Do what?"

He'd actually stepped away from her, literally physically repulsed by what he'd seen. She'd never felt more vulnerable. Arms crossed over her half-naked chest, heart beating so hard and fast she could see it thumping against her ribcage. He'd stared at her bare legs, his lip curling before he'd spoken....

And then he'd spelled it out. As if the disgust on his face hadn't been enough for her to figure out things hadn't been going the way she'd thought.

"Sleeping with you would be pity sex. And I don't do things out of pity."

Though he wasn't wearing one himself, Alex was pleased to see the smile back on Maggie's face. After he'd made his snarky comment about the snow, Maggie had fallen into a heavy silence. The kind he knew all too well. The kind that meant he'd stuck his foot in it. Again.

When Amy had died, it was as if his entire vocabulary on how to talk to people normally had been buried in the ground alongside her. It was the first time since then he felt a genuine need to change things.

Now that they were in the physio lab he'd designed from the underfloor heating up to the safety harnesses attached to the rafters, Maggie was back to being the bright, chirpy woman he'd first seen on the ferry.

"Are you sure you have the time to do this with me?"

"Absolutely. I never miss a chance to show off my second baby."

She shot him a sidelong glance as if she was reading something else into the comment then let it drop.

He hadn't meant it literally. *Obviously.* Though...he supposed building the clinic *had* been a therapy of sorts. Something to pull him and Jake out of the fug of confusion and grief they'd been swirling in ever since Amy had died. Alex knew he'd struggled. Jake had been so small when he'd lost his mother. Not even a toddler. And Alex hadn't once considered he'd be raising his son on his own.

He hadn't, of course. There had been nannies and baby-sitters and daycares—none of which had sat right with him as he'd finished his specialty in neurosurgery.

Time poor and regret rich, he'd hatched the idea to build the clinic when he'd met Cody at that conference.

Jake had a proper home now. A community. There was more "down home" daycare available than you could shake a stick at. And not just for the clinicians, for anyone on the island who needed it. Twenty-four seven.

The clinic's reputation had spread much faster than either he or Cody had expected and at the moment it seemed as though they were having to hire new people practically every week. There was a rehab specialist in England he needed to talk with. Richard...or was it Rick? Rick Fleming? Something like that. He could be a nice balance to Maggie's physio and equine therapies.

"Hey, look!" Maggie pointed at the thick crash mats at the bottom of the long flight of training stairs. "We should put some of these in your house."

Her face paled. All except for her cheeks, which turned

a hot pink. "I mean, if I'm staying at your house again. To-night. Not that I'm presuming I will be or anything. I can move to the hospital or..." She flicked her thumb toward the barn. "I bet those stairs up to the apartment aren't too bad to negotiate. Say, look at this." She spotted a pediatric posture mirror and crossed to check it out, clearly as uncomfortable discussing her living arrangements as he was.

He looked at her inspecting her own reflection then reaching out to touch the mirror.

He wanted his fingertips to be the ones meeting hers, his hand to be the one pressing against hers.

Alex took a step toward her and stopped himself.

He was her boss, not her lover.

So, this was what it felt like to be the moth drawn the flame.

To experience pure, undiluted hunger for something you knew you shouldn't touch.

He wanted her to stay at his house every bit as much as he wanted her to leave.

Perhaps if he pictured himself as one of his son's current obsessions, dinosaurs, he'd feel more resistant to her. A pterodactyl. The thick, scaly armor was far more suited to flame than the flimsy wings of a Lepidoptera. But even that made him crack a smile. The woman had him picturing himself as a pterodactyl, for crying out loud!

A flash of lightning over the ocean caught his attention. "Did you see that?"

"What?" She turned to him.

"Lightning. Out over the ocean."

"Nope. I'm too excited by all of your amazing toys." Maggie gave a little clap of her hands then twisted back and forth, soaking the facilities in as if it were a chocolate factory and not a rehab gym. It was nice to see someone so openly enthusiastic about what he'd poured so much of his life into.

She finally met his gaze. "It's like a carnival for people

on the mend. Ever thought of putting in blinking lights, spelling out 'Alex and Cody's Fun Fair' in here?"

No. He hadn't. Neither, he suspected, had Cody.

"I prefer 'Capability and Walking Lab.'"

"Lab? Okay. Where are the rats? Oh. I see. The patients are the rats. So..." She clocked his lack of smile and her own disappeared. "Lab it is, Dr. Kirkland."

She pulled her hair over her shoulder and rearranged it into a loose plait, switching to a light, bright tone, presumably to erase the *Wow, you've got a weird way of treating your patients* voice. "You two sure didn't do this by halves. Huge windows. Big, solid beams. Nice touch, hiding the steel with driftwood planks. Cuts up the whole white thing you've got going on in here." If he'd had even a hint of a smile on his face it had clearly dropped off. "Oh. Did I get that wrong? Is that vanilla cloud? The paint color on the walls?"

Maggie was obviously straining to keep the conversation going and he wasn't helping. Not with only a couple hours' worth of sleep, if he counted up the minutes here and there he must've dozed off out of sheer exhaustion.

Having Maggie just down the hall from him, tucked under the quilt his great-grandmother had made...hell, she might as well have been on the other side of his bed. The bed at the clinic on the island he wouldn't even be living on if his wife had listened to her commanding officer.

Maggie had that in her too. That selflessness that had impelled his wife to disobey orders. And he couldn't take that risk again. Not for Jake. Not for himself.

"It's just white," he said bluntly, his past colliding with his present. "Plain old, run-of-the-mill...white."

"White's actually the amalgamation of all the primary colors, so in a way you've made a bit of a color storm."

It had simply been the easiest choice.

"We— Dr. Brennan and I thought it would keep things simple." It wasn't as if building a clinic when he had still been reeling from the loss of his wife and Cody had been untangling himself from the mess of his own marriage had been easy. Choosing the perfect color palette hadn't really factored into it.

She tipped her head to the side as if trying to make herself see things his way, but the tell-tale Maggie shrug indicated she clearly didn't. Or couldn't. He lived in a world of black and white and she clearly made use of the entire color spectrum.

The decorators had actually suggested splashes of color here and there but he and Cody had thought the landscape of Maple Island provided enough visual flair without adding accent walls or murals that would detract from the work at hand. It hadn't really occurred to him that might have been the whole point.

"How long has it been open again? The clinic?"

"A year and a bit. Nearly two?" He'd lost track really. Arriving on the island three years ago. Designing and then building it. Keeping tabs on Jake. Making sure they both ate healthy food, had quality bedtime stories, and somehow trying to rediscover the fun in life. Helpfully, the bulk of the Maple Islanders saw life as one great party. There were festivals popping up all over the place. Christmas tree lightings. Long icicle contests. Gingerbread houses in storefronts, and now that the New Year was underway a whole crop of others were getting advance notice in all the storefront windows. He wasn't so sure about the vegan café's call to arms for Freeganuary. Sounded like a recipe for listeriosis to him but…he wasn't going to judge because neither did he like waste.

Which was precisely why, when he'd found out his wife had inherited an eye-watering sum she'd kept socked away "just in case", he had immediately decided to use the money to build the clinic. It had been their dream. Seeing so many soldiers return to civilian life having to deal with disabilities had drilled home their true passion. Creating a state-of-the-art rehab clinic. He just hadn't ever imagined he'd be living the dream without her.

Jake had only been a year old when her tour in Afghanistan had returned her to him in a flag-covered casket. A few days earlier she'd missed her little boy's first birthday. They'd had cupcakes from her favorite Boston bakery in a poor attempt to make it seem as if she had been there. Not that Jake had really known what was happening or remembered her calling in on a military video line that had lasted about thirty seconds before cutting out. "Mommy will be here next year," Alex had said, and then together they had blown out the solitary candle.

He tried to rub the tension out of his jaw and failed. His grief may have become manageable. But there was a bigger part of him that was still blazing with anger.

She'd been told not to disobey orders. Everyone in the military was. Before she'd left, they'd agreed parenting was to be the most important part of their lives. A direct contrast to her childhood at boarding school and his standing outside the local roadhouse, asking strangers if they wouldn't mind seeing if his mom and dad were still propping up the bar.

"I read somewhere it was your wife's legacy that paid for all this. Is that right?" Maggie asked.

He almost laughed. Amy's legacy was leaving behind a son and a husband. "Her inheritance. Yes."

He suddenly became aware that Maggie had inserted her arms into one of the support harnesses and was precariously swinging herself back and forth over the meticulously designed obstacle course.

"Please don't play with the harnesses. They're not circus swings."

"Okay." She pulled herself out of the sling and steadied it.

After a few moments of awkward silence she tried stoking the barely-there sparks of conversation. "So, I guess you're pretty much a local. Having been here...three years in total, then, is it?"

"Not so much by island standards. That takes hundreds of years, not a handful."

"Wow. Those are some standards." She rubbed her hands together and grinned as if she was accepting a challenge. Was there nothing that didn't shine with possibility in this woman's life?

He made himself say something positive so she wouldn't think he was all doom and gloom.

"You should see the place in the autumn. There's a covered bridge down the way. With the trees and leaves... and..." He swallowed. The autumn leaves looked like Maggie's hair. Wild and alive. He could almost recapture how silken it had felt as it had brushed against his cheek when he'd carried her up the stairs. He cleared his throat. "The color makes a difference."

"That's a shame. My contract's only for three months. Takes me up to the end of March."

"Ah," he said, when what he really wanted to say was, *So soon?*

She flashed him a bright smile then started pulling herself up on the small climbing wall they had for the pediatric patients. Or was it a cover for the flicker of hurt he thought he'd seen in her big brown eyes? Did she *want* to stay longer?

His ability to read people in anything other than a professional capacity had long been shot to blue blazes. So he did what came naturally and reverted to talking about work.

"You know, we're one of the first clinics in the country to put in an obstacle course like this."

"It's great," she said with utter conviction as she clambered back down the wall and began putting herself through the obstacle course with exacting movements. "I could've done with one of these. And that over there.

The multi-surface platform? Awesome. Switching from pavement to grass to gravel...they're all challenges people learning to walk again have to face, and to be able to do it with this great sling? Amazing." They both looked up at the tracks that ran the length of the two-story lab and then back at each other.

"Glad it suits." Anything would suit her. A set of scrubs. The athletic gear she wore now. *Nothing.*

He pressed his fingers against his eyes, trying to erase the picture of Maggie in his shower, and failed.

"Yup." Maggie nodded, taking a scan of the area. "It's all...very...clean."

So he gave her a little lecture on the importance of hygiene. As if she didn't already know the essentials of it. Yet another open-mouth-insert-foot moment to chalk up on the Alex Isn't Actually Human board.

Once they'd finished up in the walking lab, he showed her to the hydrotherapy center.

"I suppose this is the 'buoyancy and aquatic submersion lab'?" She waved her hands in the style of a New York showgirl.

"No," he continued dryly. "We went out on a ledge with this one and call it the hydrotherapy center."

She laughed then gave the place a second look. "It's big. Hey!" Her brown eyes lit up with excitement. "This'd be a fun place to have a pool party in the winter."

"Or perhaps rehabilitate patients who've suffered life-altering injuries."

That one earned him A Look.

Not judgmental. More as if she were trying to find the place where all his uptight responses were coming from. Figure out what made him tick. He suspected her patients saw a lot of The Look.

It was strangely powerful.

He felt a pounding against his chest, like his soul had

been kept prisoner and was trying to break free now that he'd found someone so unbelievably…right.

And wrong.

He wasn't all rules and regulations this, or rip off the silver lining that. Hell's bells. Old Alex would've pulled off his shirt, grabbed Maggie's hand and jumped in the pool right this very minute. With a whoop.

A pool he wouldn't have if his wife wasn't dead.

Precisely why his responsible self had been forced to take over. He had a son to look after. Patients to protect. So, yeah. "New Alex" certainly wasn't as fun as the man he'd once been, but at least he was alive.

Which was, he realized with the swift cruelty of a knife entering the gut, not remotely the same thing as *living*.

His phone buzzed in his pocket. He turned away from Maggie and stared out the window at the thickening snow while he took the call.

Work. That's what gave him structure. The framework of the clinic enabled him to make sure Jake had a reliable, safe childhood. He didn't need any flame-haired daredevils poking away at parts of himself he'd long since locked away.

"I'm afraid we've got a slip and fall arriving at the hospital. One of the Brady kids."

Maggie's eyebrows scrunched together then arrowed up. They were very expressive eyebrows.

"A suspected fractured wrist."

"Youch. Out in the snow?"

"Outside the bakery. Apparently there was some sliding on the ice going on and 'mayhem ensued.'" He was quoting their receptionist, Marlee. She was a Brady by birth and the auntie of Tom Junior, known to all as Tommy. Or was it Tina? Three years and he still hadn't straightened out the four Brady kids. Obviously, he knew the difference between the boys and the girls but Billy, Brigid, Tommy and Tina had all spent their fair share of time in the clinic's various exam rooms. Bright orange hair and clear blue eyes. Each and every one of them. Even the family dog. An Irish setter. What else?

"Remind me who the Bradys are again?"

"Tom and Fiona Brady run the island's more...traditional bakery."

"With the apple pie?"

"Precisely."

"Ha! I love the way you say that all slow and southern. I feel like I'm in a costume drama."

He furrowed his brow.

Maggie skipped over his lack of response and tossed him a new question. "What's an *un*traditional bakery?"

"Oh, you know, all of that chia seed and goji berry nonsense."

"You think nutritious food is nonsense?"

He smiled. She was obviously a super-foods fan. Most athletes were. "No. Not really. The only time I truly protest about the island's vegan café is when a leaden lump of mashed-up dates is sold with a mandatory sage smudging and passed off as a brownie."

She barked with laughter, pointed her fingers at him as if they were little pistols and made the clicking sound one usually made to tell a horse to get a move on. "Gotcha. When it's an affront to actual taste buds." She abruptly pulled a confused face. "Isn't a slip and fall a bit below your pay grade?"

He clapped his hands together and rubbed them. Now, *this* was something he could enthuse about. "Not in the slightest. It's one of the reasons we structured the clinic the way we did. We wanted to be part of a community. So to do that we also care for the community."

"Sounds great. Mind if I tag along?"

He stiffened.

She read his mind. "If I promise to adhere to the boundaries of safety and health regulations?"

He stuffed his phone back in his pocket. "Fine."

CHAPTER SEVEN

MAGGIE WORKED HER way back to the central reception desk while Alex jogged off to make sure the imaging room was set up. He told her to meet and greet the patient and he'd find them.

The front desk was run by a woman with an amazing swirl of orange plaits circling her head, but there wasn't as much as a glimpse of Alex disappearing into an exam room.

"You must be Maggie Green. I'm Marlee Paynter. I had a peek at your file and I was thrilled to see there was another redhead joining the team." She glanced at a colorful wall calendar beside her. "You're a week early, aren't you?"

"Long story." She gave her a quick rundown of the twins, the transfer, the decision to come early, leaving out the part about her ex being the spur in her side. "Alex seems all right with it."

It was a lie that would fly, as her father used to say.

Marlee gave her a quick scan then tutted. "Looks like Cody hasn't managed to get you all sorted out with the Maple Clinic gear yet. Sweatshirts, winter jacket and whatnot?"

"I haven't met with Cody yet."

"No?" She tutted again. "I suppose he would've been out with his children when all of the kerfuffle was going on with Salty yesterday." She shook her head. "Honest to goodness. A couple of brainboxes, the pair of them, but did either of them come equipped with meet-and-greet skills?" She didn't pause for an answer. "Did Alex get you a security pass? It allows you into the storerooms, staffroom, secret nap room that we all know about. That sort of thing."

Maggie shook her head.

"That man…" She rolled her eyes and clicked her tongue again. "Oh, c'mon over here, honey. You are a tiny little thing, aren't you? Let me give you a Maple Island welcome. We're huggers. Apart from Old Salty, of course, but I suppose that goes without saying. I hope you're not averse?"

"Not in the slightest!" Maggie let herself be enveloped in a big old bear hug. Marlee smelled of sugar cookies and frosting. "Whoops!" She reached out to steady herself on Marlee's ample arms.

"Did I knock you off center, honey?"

"Oh, that's easily done." Maggie lifted up her trouser legs and showed off her prosthetics.

Marlee let out a low whistle. "Well, I never." She snapped her fingers. "Of course. Maggie Green of sporting fame. Equestrian, wasn't it? A bit of running too?"

Maggie nodded.

She felt someone approach behind her.

"Two golds and a fistful of silver medals behind her."

Mercy. Her tummy flipped. Alex really had been trawling the internet.

Marlee gave her forehead a theatrical *thunk*. "Can't believe I didn't put two and two together. Must be that cold front blowing in. Total brain freeze if you step outside." She let out a whoop. "You can be Maple Island's very own Calamity Jane! Is it all right if I call you that? Calamity Maggie?"

Maggie winced, wishing the words Calamity and Maggie didn't go quite so hand in hand, but she had to admit, which she did, that it would be a pretty accurate moniker.

"I think Miss Green or plain old Maggie would be more appropriate, Marlee."

Marlee laughed and shook her head. "Okay, Dr. Kirkland. Whatever you say."

"Any sign of the patient?" Alex looked at Marlee, eyebrows raised in a silent query.

"It's Billy. He was the one down helping with Salty's boat yesterday." Marlee continued unabated. "Well, this is just wonderful, *Miss Green*. I'm going to tell my brother, Tom, who runs the bistro and bakery, that you're here and mark my words—there will be a breakfast scramble named after you in no time flat."

Maggie full on belly laughed at that one. "Well, tell him to make sure there are lots of jalapeños in it. I like things hot and spicy." Maggie felt Alex's gaze land on her with a thud. She backpedaled as quickly as she could, doing her best to ignore the heat creeping into her cheeks. "And hash browns," she added. "Plain old potatoes sure are good too."

Oh, jinks. Here she was, on a babble-a-thon again!

Marlee peered at her inquisitively, then Alex. They both developed avid interests in looking at anything other than Marlee, whose attention was caught by something happening out front. "There are the boys pulling up now." She pointed at Maggie. "Make sure you pop by the desk later, honey, and I'll get you sorted with all of the sweatshirts and things."

"Thanks. That'd be great." She meant it, too.

"Anything complicated? Want me to have a look?"

Cody stuck his head into the imaging lab.

"Nothing that requires surgery, if that's what you're asking." Alex pushed his wheelie chair back from the screens to give Cody room...almost grateful to have someone between himself and Maggie. As ridiculous as it sounded, he suddenly understood what all those shampoo commercials were talking about. Her hair smelled amazing. *She* smelled amazing. If he hadn't already made a big show of having her shadow him, he would've handed her over to Cody right there and then.

"Looks like a straight-up distal radius fracture to me. Undisplaced." His friend frowned.

"Normally that's good news, Cody."

Cody clearly didn't even hear his lame attempt at humor and leaned in for a closer look at the anteroposterior X-ray. "Is that—?"

"Yup." Alex nodded. "He's fractured the ulna as well. Hairline."

"Standard stuff for a..." They all looked toward the X-ray room, where Billy was currently trying to fix his hair in the one-way window. "How old is this one?"

"Can none of you tell the Bradys apart?" Maggie laughed. "This one's Billy, remember. He's fourteen."

"Fourteen going on twenty-seven." Alex checked his tone. It wasn't as if he'd been *jealous* of the non-stop flirting Billy was unleashing each time Maggie was in the room with him. More... He checked himself again. The boy was a boy. He was a man. The kiss had been an anomaly. Maggie was a colleague. And this was work.

"Want me to set it?" Cody looked at his watch. "I said I'd pick up the kids in half an hour but it shouldn't take long."

"No, no." Alex stood up and nodded at Maggie. "Just a standard sugar-tong splint, yeah?" Cody nodded. "You go on ahead and pick up the girls. Maggie can assist me."

Maggie smiled at him as if it were a given that they were a team.

The shot of warmth that burst open in his chest was the total opposite of a professional response.

Good grief. This whole shadowing thing might be a serious mistake.

"Right!" He held the door open for her. "Guess we'd better let Billy the Kid know his ice-hockey career is on hold for the next six weeks."

A couple of minutes later he was pulling the splint, padding material and a handful of other supplies out of a cupboard as Maggie got Billy settled onto a stool adjacent to the exam table.

"So, Maggie." She'd obviously dispensed with the Miss Green moniker and Billy clearly hadn't finished with his twenty questions. "Do you think a broken wrist warrants some equine therapy?"

She nodded soberly. "Can you just prop your elbow up here? And, yes, there is definitely some equine therapy *post*-splinting and *post*-confirmation that the fracture has healed."

Alex tuned in to their conversation. He'd never heard of horse riding as a therapeutic follow-up to a broken wrist.

The teenage boy sat bolt upright, a smile lighting up his face. "Seriously? What type?"

"I call it the catch and release therapeutic method. You start a week or so after the cast is off. It's a wonderful strength builder."

Alex arched an eyebrow. He'd not heard of that. Sure, equine therapy wasn't his specialty, but...catch and release? Sounded like fishing terminology to him.

Grip. Rotation. Motion. Strength. Function. Those were more along the lines of the terminology he was used to using.

Billy leaned forward on the stool, cradling his wrist in his other hand. "What does that involve? Lassoing the horses or something? Wrestling them to the ground? That sort of thing?"

"It's a little different than that... Elbow back on the table, please, young man. Can I get you to put your arm at a forty-five-degree angle, please? Yup. Good. Just like that. You can get paid for it, too."

"What? The therapy? Result! What d'you have to do?"

Alex turned around just in time to catch Maggie miming a shoveling motion.

Billy groaned. "You mean shoveling horse poop out of the stables? Not a chance, sister."

Maggie laughed. She'd clearly been expecting the less-than-enthusiastic response. "It's a good job. I did it for years to earn my spending money."

"I'm only fourteen." Billy made a noise suggesting her job proposal was akin to child labor.

"So was I when I started. Keep your wrist and hand up, please, my friend."

Interesting. Many parents would've been as protective as hell about a double amputee in close quarters with a horse.

"Well, then." She nodded toward Alex. "I suspect Dr. Kirkland has some much more useful advice for you if you want to get back out to the rink as soon as possible."

Nice way to segue into the actual medical advice.

Before he could start talking about finger movement and how six weeks was the bare minimum of recovery time, Billy continued, "Oh, there isn't a hockey rink here. I was practicing my skids on Main Street."

Interesting. His father had told them it was a plain slip and fall that had caused the accident.

Alex hid his smile at the sink as he filled a basin with warm water. He didn't think he'd ever extracted this much information from a patient before. No wonder his invitations into town had dried up after the first few months here. He didn't *talk* to people.

Maggie patted the exam table. "Elbow back here, pal, or I'm going to have to clamp it down. How cool is that about the rink?"

"No. There isn't a rink." Billy tried to wriggle his fingers and winced with pain. "The sidewalk in front of the bakery was frozen and my brother Tommy and I were having a skidding war before we salted them down."

"Sounds fun," Maggie said.

"Sounds like something that leads to a fractured wrist."

They both stared at Alex with expressions that made it clear he'd just rained on their parade.

Well, it was true.

"How about we get this splint on?"

Maggie shot him a curious look. One that obviously wondered why fun and work couldn't go hand in hand.

It was a good question.

A few of hours later, after they'd completed the tour and the rest of Alex's rounds, the pair of them stood outside the twins' room. Alex scanned their charts as Rosaline looked on. The Haitian nurse's expression was as calm and relaxed as ever. Nothing ever seemed to ruffle her feathers.

"As I said, Dr. Kirkland, nothing of note today. Just the usual R&R."

"Rest and relaxation?" asked Maggie.

"Rest and recovery," corrected Rosaline. "This is gonna be one of those cases that gets under your skin."

"No doubt." Maggie fist-bumped Rosaline. He saw an instant kinship blossom right in front of him.

Alex shook his head in wonder. He'd never seen Rosaline do anything remotely hip. How did Maggie know to do these things?

"Poor little things without their parents here." Maggie poked her head around the corner at the children, who were watching a film on the ceiling-mounted television they could tilt to whatever angle suited the patient's eyeline.

His heart went out to her. She must've spent weeks if not months in and out of hospital after her own illness. Years of rehab. A lifetime really. Her "problem" would never go away, unlike these kids.

Most people who'd been through what she had would run for the hills when it came to a hospital-based profession. Seeing patients achieve what she never could. The strength of character she must possess…

"Dr. Kirkland?" Rosaline was giving him a funny look. "You have been in touch with the parents, right?"

"Yes. Absolutely. If the weather forecasts are anything to go by, and we now know they're not…" he threw a quick glance at Maggie, who gave a confirming nod of the head "…the replacement ferry is going to be up and running again in a couple of days. We can always get a helicopter from Boston Harbor to bring them over. Gratis."

Rosaline gave him one of her sidelong knowing looks. The one that said she knew he had a soft spot for certain patients, even though he claimed to treat them all the same.

She was right. The Walsh children's case had hit a nerve with him. Two parents trying to provide a bit of holiday magic with what little means they had and just like that, in a single terrifying moment, their children's lives had changed. He was going to do everything in his power to make sure those two kids walked out of here with their heads held high.

"Before we go in, shall we have a quick recap?"

The women nodded. As if they had a choice. "Peyton's SCI is the more severe of the two. Each twin's spinal cord received a short, sharp blow when the loose scaffolding fell on them, the velocity of the poles only hindered by the wooden porch."

Rosaline and Maggie nodded. They knew what he was really saying. The twins were lucky to be alive at all.

The emergency treatment they had received from the paramedics out of Boston Harbor had been exemplary. Somehow they'd managed to maintain blood pressure, which was crucial to keeping blood flow along the spinal cord. Dr. Rafael Valdez had been a bit of a revelation as well. The Spanish doctor had already been on the periphery of Alex's radar. He was a relatively new hire at Boston Harbor, and he'd come up trumps with these two.

"Peyton needed removal of bone fragments and stabilization for her fractured thoracic T11 and T12 as well as her L1 vertebrae."

"And the Brown-Sequard syndrome," Maggie interjected.

"Just getting to that." It complicated things. A lot. "When Peyton suffered a penetrating injury from the end of a broken plank that had been part of the scaffolding walkway, it resulted in Brown-Sequard syndrome. In other words, one side of the spinal cord was damaged with neurological implications. Luckily, Dr. Valdez was able to extract the multiple shards of wood splintered in her thoracic spine and stop the leaching of spinal fluid. Had he not done that she would very likely have faced partial if not complete paralysis."

He flicked to another set of notes on his tablet then looked up, about to launch into another detailed ream of stats.

Maggie, he saw, had her sponge face on again. He shook away the moniker. He needed to come up with another term. She wasn't spongy in the slightest. She was... absorbed. Engaged. Interested. Completely committed. Just as she had been the moment his lips had touched hers.

He cleared his throat, looked at his tablet and continued.

"Connor is a bit better off. He received a single solitary blow from the scaffolding and had two incomplete vertebral fractures at L3 and L4." Connor had, ironically enough, been the recipient of a ground-breaking surgery involving "mini-scaffolding" that was behaving as a three-dimensional bandage until his vertebrae were fully healed.

"So, basically we need to get the motor signals in the spinal column up and running so we can teach these kids how to walk again," Maggie said thoughtfully.

He smiled and nodded. It was a nice way to boil down an extremely complicated medical scenario. He was impressed. Yet again. She had a canny knack for taking on incredibly detailed, complex medical information and cutting through to the quick of the matter. Very useful for talking to patients.

"They're young. Healthy, apart from the obvious." He nodded toward the walking lab. "If all goes well, we'll have them there in a couple of months."

"No better place for these children to be." Rosaline gave Maggie another fist bump. "This is the place science and miracles collide."

A smile bloomed on Maggie's lips. "Nice. I like that." Her eyes glittered as she looked across at Alex. "Did you come up with that?"

"I'm not much of a believer in miracles."

She made a derisive noise that said what Rosaline was muttering. "Surprise, surprise."

So he was a science guy. Miracles were—miracles were scooping gorgeous redheads up and into your arms without so much as a thought as to how intimate it would feel. Only to compound the sensuality of the moment by getting into the shower with her...watching her undress. Feeling every muscle in his body ache to pull her to him—then do it. And kiss her as if he were a man who'd just crawled out of the desert and she was the oasis. Yup. Unless you counted any of that, he was definitely a science guy all the way.

Otherwise he'd have to chalk up his son's arrival as divine intervention. And letting go of her? That had been pure, straight-up hell.

A twinge of guilt lanced his conscience. When he'd tucked Jake in last night, his son had asked about his mother. Alex had murmured something noncommittal in return, given him a kiss then left his son's room as quickly as possible, unable to match up the feelings he was having for Maggie with the ones he'd had for Amy.

What he felt when he looked at Maggie was something entirely different than what he'd experienced with Amy. He'd been young then. Driven. Looking forward because looking back had been too painful.

All he'd done in the past six years was look back. But with Maggie?

She was...invigorating. Refreshing. Life-affirming. She made him think about tomorrow. And the day after that. And it scared the hell out of him.

"You okay, Doc?"

"Of course." Alex gave a little laugh to prove it. Rosaline quirked an eyebrow at him, making it clear she didn't buy it.

"I'll leave you two to it, then, Dr. Kirkland. I'm just going to go check on Salty. See if he's reduced anyone else to tears recently."

"Good luck with that." Maggie laughed. "Nice to meet you, Rosaline."

"You too, honey. Wonderful to have someone on the team who brings a smile to this man's face."

Alex and Maggie stared at each other.

She was gone before Alex could protest. He'd smiled before he'd met Maggie.

"Shall we go say hi to the twins?"

His shoulders dropped away from his ears as Maggie went in and began her usual bubbly chatter with the children. From the sound of their squeals you'd have thought they hadn't seen each other for a year.

Maybe it was a show? Maggie doing her best to ignore Rosaline's comment as diligently as he was? If that was the case, they'd get along just fine.

Oh, you get along a whole lot more than fine.

And therein lay the crux of the matter.

Sure, it had been less than twenty-four hours since he'd met her, but he'd known in fewer than a handful that he'd ask Amy to marry him one day.

Look how well that had turned out.

You have a beautiful boy. A son. If you hadn't taken a risk, you wouldn't have Jake.

He leant against the doorframe and watched Maggie as

she did a few non-traditional shadow puppets on the wall to crack the twins up. It worked.

Acknowledging these feelings, admitting his attraction, facing up to the fact Maggie had blasted into his life, kicked open the door to his heart and jammed her foot in it... If he faced up to all those things, owned them? It meant moving on. And he wasn't sure he would ever be ready for that. Staying angry with Amy...well, he guessed it kept the grief at bay.

Thank goodness he hadn't made a New Year's resolution list. Sorting out six years of fastidiously ignored emotions was more than enough to confront. Or he could do what he usually did—ignore it all and carry on as he was doing. Life was fine. Jake was fine. The patients were fine. Everything was fine.

Fine isn't enough. Is it?

He forced himself to tune into the conversation the twins were having with Maggie.

"How 'bout this place, huh? Totally worth yesterday's drama, am I right?"

They said something he couldn't quite make out.

"What?" She stared at both of them, then shook her head. "No way. Dr. Alex is *super*-nice. Sometimes he talks like a butler, but that's just because his brains are so big. Trust me." She made an exaggerated cross over her heart. "He is absolutely the best man to help you both get on over to the rehab gym where we can use all of their cool gadgets, yeah?" She glanced over at Alex, a hint of uncertainty in her gaze. She knew her style was totally different from his. But that's what this whole exercise was about—seeing patients together. Seeing if their styles...meshed. His heart started hammering against his chest. It was clearly in cahoots with his soul. Asking for another chance to show what it could do.

First up? He'd show the kids he was more than an uptight butler. Mind you, Jeeves was a damn sight better than Dr. Protocol.

"Right, kiddos. Rosaline will be back shortly if you need her, but in the meantime you two rest up real good, y'hear?" Alex said heartily.

Since when was he talking southern again?

No points for that one.

Maggie was beaming at the children. "See? Doesn't he have a great accent? No one can be boring when they talk like that. You should hear him say 'apple pie.'"

Their eyes met and held tight.

"Apple pie."

He was rewarded with cheers from the three of them.

Despite himself, he grinned, and performed a little bow. "Happy to be of service to y'all."

They cheered again.

Funny. He'd always made a point of hiding his accent. As if it betrayed the fact he was human. Had a past. Had feelings.

Maggie dropped kisses on each of the children's foreheads. "Enjoy the rest of your movie and I'll see you soon, okay?"

A chorus of "Goodbye" and "See you soon" rang through the room. The complete opposite from how things normally were. Quiet. Serene. Scientific.

The funny thing was, as he and Maggie headed toward their next patient, he caught himself whistling.

CHAPTER EIGHT

"I DON'T THINK he's ready."

Maggie dug her heels in. "I think he can handle it."

Nothing like a stand-off with the boss about a patient to test the whole *Let's see how we work together* thing. Especially when all Maggie could think about was kissing him.

It had been nearly seventy-two hours since she'd arrived on the island—not that she was counting—and still her lips were reliving those kisses as if they'd just parted.

She scrunched the thoughts into a corner of her brain and tried again. "This *is* why you hired me, remember? To do equine therapy."

Alex's body language screamed defensiveness. Arms crossed, posture ramrod straight, green eyes at half-mast. She got it. His clinic. His ground-breaking methods. His rules. And yet...she still wanted to reach out to him. Touch him. Soothe away his rigid my-way-or-the-highway vibe. Show him she had a different way of looking at things that could bring out something new in a patient.

They opted for a staring contest.

Had she noticed how long and jet black his lashes were before?

Damn long and inky black was the answer to that one.

She mirrored his own body language to see if that helped.

"No horses. Not today."

Okay, so that hadn't worked. She dropped the crossed-arms pose. Even when he was telling her no his voice was lovely. Like a late-night radio chat show host who lulled you to sleep.

She put on her best professional voice to try another tack to make her point. "In my opinion, I think the patient is best served if we approach their weak points head on. Getting Mark out to the barn is a great way to do that."

"Mark has plenty of things to work on in the ability lab."

Alex's program was great. No surprise there. The thing was, she found it *much* easier to get a read on a patient's emotional well-being if she saw them interact with the horses. The four-legged therapists had a sixth sense about people and the way they responded to a patient and vice versa revealed much more than a simple sit-down chat could.

She swallowed the slew of examples she wanted to parade in front of Alex and put on a smile instead. He liked facts. Order. "So. What we've got here is an army veteran. Retired, disabled at thirty-five with PTSD. But that's not why he's here. He's recovering from a stroke and is learning to walk again. Hopefully without the double set of canes that he is currently using."

"Which is why he should be heading over to the walking lab." Alex made one of those faces that said he was obviously in the right.

"Absolutely. But..." she brandished her index finger "...not until I observe him with a horse."

"For what purpose?"

"A number of things. I want to see if he will take the opportunity to walk there for one. If getting out of the hospital and into a barn is a big enough incentive. Two, in the lab he's going to be on high alert. Anxious. He's got depression, right?"

Alex nodded. "We have a psychiatrist on the team. Two of them, in fact."

"But you don't have anyone doing equine therapy with them. I'd be more than happy to team up with a therapist while I do the physio." She held up a hand as Alex parted those perfect lips of his and kept on talking. "Three, I don't even want to put Mark on a horse today. I just want to see how the horse responds to him and vice versa."

"What's that going to tell you?"

She looked him straight in the eye and said, "What's inside."

It was one of the most powerful tools she had. She met people at their most vulnerable and the way they approached a horse told her a dozen things about the patient right off. If they were scared. Angry. Weighted with grief. Come to think of it, she wouldn't mind seeing Alex down at the barn with a horse.

Alex put on a voice that sounded an awful lot like he was placating a spoiled child. "We know you'd planned on doing a bit of riding with a handful of patients, but I think for today it would be best if you just stick to the proto— To the plan," he hastily corrected himself.

She fought the urge to grin because this wasn't about teasing Alex. It was about what was best for a patient.

"I am sticking to the plan. My patient? *My plan.*" She pressed the heels of her trainers into the floor and pushed herself up as straight as she could. Her eyeline hit his shoulders. They were all big and broad and strong and ridiculously distracting when she was trying to make a proper, professional point. Not everyone took to her "free range" approach at first, but she found it delivered results.

"Look, Maggie, I am not trying to rain on your parade."
Yes, you are.

Alex tightened his lips as if he'd read her mind. Whoops.

"I am merely trying to maintain the highest level of treatment and I'm not ready to send someone running off to the barns with you on their first appointment."

"How about…" Maggie smiled and half turned toward

Mark's door "...instead of this being a session where I shadow you, you shadow me?"

"Hang on a minute."

Maggie frowned as he held up a hand to stop her.

She stared at it hard.

He dropped it.

"I've spent the last few days being a good little shadow, right? I get it. I needed to learn how things work here and now that I've seen your bells and whistles and have a pretty solid hand on them..."

He gave an incredulous snort.

She chose to ignore it. "...it's time to show you some of my bells and whistles."

He arched an eyebrow.

"As it were." She smirked then went dead serious. "Listen, Mark is going to be my patient, right?"

Alex nodded.

"You know as well as I do that the first appointment is critical for establishing rapport. If I go in there using someone else's treatment plan I'm going to seem awkward. Uncomfortable. Your way is amazing. For you. My way works great, too. For me. I spent all of yesterday afternoon in the barns and the horses you have are amazing. Here's your chance to see them in action." She took a step back as if to give him physical space to consider what she'd said.

He scrubbed at his jaw and shook his head. "We understood you were going to do *some* equine therapy but that the bulk of your practice would be indoors, in the labs, the pool. That sort of thing."

She grimaced. "Who gave you that impression?"

Alex was just about to say Cody had when he remembered all Cody had mentioned to him about Maggie was that he was hiring her. He'd filled in all of the blanks he'd wanted to. If he was going to treat her like any of their other staff, he'd hear her out. Do as she suggested.

"Fine." He held out an arm as if ushering her into Mark's room…like a butler. "I'd be delighted to observe."

An hour later he genuinely was. He knew exactly what Maggie had been talking about when she'd quoted Winston Churchill at the pair of them when Mark had pulled one of the horse's big heads toward his own and they'd stood there in silence for several moments, forehead to forehead, as if they were healing one another.

"'There is something about the outside of a horse that is good for the inside of a man,'" Maggie had quoted, steady and low. She knew her crowd. It took a military man to know one. And, it seemed, a Maggie.

Mark had enjoyed the session, too, which was more to the point. For the first time since he'd entered the clinic over two weeks ago, Mark Segal had finished a session with a smile.

They'd even saluted one another and agreed to meet at the walking lab at the crack of dawn the next day.

Irritation that he hadn't been able to achieve the same results pulsed through him until he remembered there were multiple ways to skin a cat. His just happened to be the version one could publish in medical journals.

An urge to kick something—namely himself—took hold of him something fierce. Since when had he become so damned stuffy?

Since his world had been knocked off its very boring axis by her.

"Right!" Maggie turned to him, an element of bravura to her posture as she faced him directly. "What did you make of that?"

"I thought it was terrific."

Surprise charged all her features, quickly followed by disbelief. "You did?"

"Absolutely. Walking to the barn with him was an excellent way to diagnose where he stood in terms of motor skills, balance, co-ordination. The way you described to him how riding a horse would help synchronize his neurological and motor skills was concise, clear. It set a goal I don't think he'd seen as possible before."

"I'm glad you were there to see it." If he wasn't mistaken, a hit of pride pinked up her cheeks. "Horses are prey animals. And so are humans. We have to feel each other out, see whether or not it's safe to approach." She glanced up at him then quickly looked away.

"Is that—?" He realized he was treading on personal territory here. Vastly uncomfortable terrain. He took the step anyway. "Is that how you thought of people after you had meningitis?"

"After I had the double amputation, you mean?"

He nodded. Impressed. She didn't dance around things as he had a tendency to do when he wasn't discussing things professionally.

She considered the question for a minute, eyes up, brows raised, a solitary finger tracing the outline of her lips...

Her eyes flicked to his and he knew in an instant that she saw he wasn't thinking about the finer points of emotional recovery from a double amputation.

She shrugged, her go-to move to lighten the atmosphere. Make his question less of a *thing*. "I don't think I went that deep and heavy in my thought process. I was drawn to the fact that horses instinctually know who to trust. I guess I wish I had that skill too."

He was about to say she could trust him but when he saw dark memories skate across her eyes like shadows, he bit it back.

Someone had hurt her straight through to the heart. Someone she hadn't realized couldn't be trusted.

She pulled her tablet out and began tabbing through it.

A desire rose in him to be the man who changed that. Who showed her that being able to trust someone was possible. That she didn't always have to be bright and smiley and optimistic. That it was okay to let other people see she was human. That someone would be there for her when feelings roared up from the darker side of the emotional spectrum. Fear. Pain. Grief.

Was that someone him?

He shook his head.

He didn't know. These were all things he probably could've done with hearing when Amy had died. A surge of protectiveness for Maggie washed through him like a healing balm. Maybe this was why she had come into his life. Why it felt like she was yanking him out of his emotional comfort zone. She had an instinct that it was time for him to let go of his rigid attachment to protocol. Something he'd convinced himself he needed in order to give his son a good life. A happy life.

Maggie looked up from her tablet. "Shall we alternate now? You take the lead on one, I take the next?"

"That sounds acceptable."

She smirked at him, gave a quick salute and mouthed, "Okay, Jeeves!" before scanning through her newly assigned tablet to find their next patient.

This time her teasing pleased him. Bringing a smile to her face was far better than raising those worry lines across her forehead. He vowed then and there to be someone Maggie could trust. Implicitly.

Even if it did come at the cost of his own dignity. And once again, as he turned to follow in Maggie's energetic wake, he found himself whistling as he worked.

"I think three stitches should do the trick."

The young mother covered her face in horror. "I only turned away for a second."

"Sometimes it only takes a second, Annabelle. Best to keep an eye on an energetic little boy like this at all times, or remove anything that could cause injury."

Don't sound so sharp. Accidents happen.

Alex gave the knee of the toddler on the exam table a little rub, doing his best to ignore Maggie's horrified expression. He knew his bedside manner appalled her. She was all sunshine and possibility and he was all about making sure his patients knew how to avoid another incident in the future. Safety first. Sunshine later. As long as you had the proper SPF.

"Not too long now, Jim."

"It's Stefan," Annabelle corrected him.

"Of course." Alex shook his head. He normally wasn't this awful. This stiff. Having Maggie shadow him the last few days had him on edge. When she looked at him, he could almost feel her physically teasing apart everything that made him tick. He was perfectly happy with how he had been ticking for the past few years, thank you very much.

He fixed Stefan with a tight smile. He knew he could be more jocular with the patients. More buddy-buddy. But it simply wasn't his style.

The odd smile and "There, there" was the best he could rustle up with Maggie staring at him like she was. All wide-eyed and *Okay, boss.*

She's not like that, you idiot. She's just better at talking to people than you are.

"I need to get the suture kit out and I'll do my best to patch you up like a little pirate." Stefan began to cry.

He had a boy of his own, for heaven's sake! He knew how to talk to children. What was *wrong* with him?

Annabelle settled her son then turned to Maggie. "I was making his sandwich. Peanut butter and jelly. His favorite. He walked into the one little bit of the counter I hadn't managed to toddler-proof."

"It's like they have magnets drawing them straight to the danger zone, isn't it?" Maggie gave Annabelle a quick sideways hug. "He'll be fine. Alex is an amazing whizz with stitches. Aren't you, Alex?" She shot him a grin and just like that he felt his pride stir again.

How did she do that?

"And then..." She crossed to the exam table while Alex was getting the suture kit in order and walked a couple of her fingers up Stefan's legs then gave him a little tickle, which he adored—*obviously*. "Dr. Alex is going to get your face all gorgeous, and you and your mom can both rest easy."

And just like that, harmony was restored.

He gave his head a little shake and smiled. Maggie Green was clearly an asset to the team. To his sanity? Probably not. But patients came first here. He'd just have to find a way to cope with all these fresh stirrings he was feeling when she was about, otherwise Dr. Protocol would become known as Dr. Pain-in-the-Posterior, and for the first time in a long time he cared about making a good impression.

Maggie stopped and listened as they came out of the exam room once they'd tidied up.

"Is that...? Are those...? Have we gone to war?"

"It's the Boston Harbor helicopter." Alex nodded toward the front of the clinic. "There was a window in the weather so Dr. Valdez has flown in to check on the twins."

"Rafael Valdez? He's such an incredible surgeon. I love him. You guys should totally hire him. Offer him anything. Give him my barn apartment if you have to!" Maggie enthused, then immediately regretted it. From the look on Alex's face, one didn't gush about other surgeons here. Or suggest they give up apartments that meant she'd be totally reliant on the room in her boss's home. "Or not." She gave her head a scratch. "Obviously, you'll do what you think is best."

"Obviously."

She hid her smile behind her hand. If Alex didn't have that slow southern drawl going on, she would've sworn he was actually British. All proper and concise and, now that she'd seem him work with quite a few patients, incredibly good at his job.

A few minutes later she was even more impressed by him. She'd already had to duck into the twins' bathroom three times to hide her tears.

Dr. Valdez hadn't just brought himself. He'd brought the twins' parents and the reunion was the kind of thing that brought immediate tears to her eyes. But Alex? He kept his grip on reality just as he always seemed to.

"You should be proud of the twins," she heard him saying as she stemmed her sniffles and returned to the main room. "They've both been healing well. Listening to doctor's orders."

"I listen to them better," Connor said. "Because I'm older," he added before Peyton could protest.

"I can hear just as well as you can," Peyton shot back. "I just have to do different exercises. Maggie said the way I wiggled my toes was amazing."

"She said the way I wiggled *my* toes was brilliant!"

Maggie giggled and gave the twins' parents an apologetic shrug. "We had a toe-wiggling contest. It was pretty incredible." She wagged her finger at the twins. "The two of you are forgetting I said you were *both* the winners."

"I'm going to be the first one to ride a horse," Connor told his father.

"I'm going to be the first one to swim in the pool." Peyton cut in.

"Hush, you two! The doctors will think we raised you like wolves!" Katie, their mother, gently admonished them.

"A healthy spirit of competition is a huge help as far as I'm concerned."

Maggie bit down on the inside of her cheek when Alex shot her a dubious look.

"It just means they'll work harder. Doesn't it, kids?"

They both cheered then started singing, "We Are the Champions."

Aaron and Katie Walsh beamed at their children. They were clearly so relieved they'd passed the immediate danger of the accident. Listening to their children bicker was actually the beautiful sound of life. Of recovery. All of which made Maggie tear up again. She turned away, swiped at her cheeks then glanced at her watch.

"Ooh! Is that the time?"

Alex gave her a curious look.

"I told Jake I would make my super-duper stir-fry tonight. If that's okay with you."

Alex did a quick scan around the room to check everyone's response. Maggie wasn't being very discreet about their housing arrangements. It wasn't like it was a secret, but...had the woman never heard the saying, "Be discreet in all things"? The Duke of Wellington had said it. Or something like it.

In truth, no one seemed all that bothered about what Maggie had said except for him.

Dr. Valdez hadn't even noticed and was asking Maggie about her rehab plans whilst the Walshes were busy talking with the twins about how long they would be staying—just for the day this time—when they would come back—as soon as possible—and whether they could stay for a long time then—they thought so, but they'd have to ask Alex about housing arrangements.

He shook his head and silently admonished himself. *Lighten up, man. The whole world won't change if a woman goes into your kitchen and makes a stir-fry.*

It will if you walk into the shower with her again.

Precisely why he'd started setting his alarm an hour early. He was downstairs, making porridge, when she showered. No chance of walking in, pulling her into his arms and kissing her stupid again.

He gave a solid nod. See? Calm. Controlled. Totally able to put the past behind him. Perfect.

An hour later, Alex and Rafael were giving the Walshes a bit of alone time with the twins before they headed off. They stood in the glass breezeway that looked out over the central courtyard.

"So, you'll consider joining us, then?" Alex had had a quick chat with Cody, who had agreed they should green-light an offer for Rafael to join them at the clinic.

Rafael nodded. "Absolutely. The daycare situation would really help me." He ran a hand through his hair. A gesture Alex knew well. The worried dad head scrub. "Gracie needs special care. For her condition."

"Autism, isn't it?" Alex asked. He gave Rafael a sympathetic clap on the shoulder. It was already tough, being a single parent. Doing it when your child required extra care made it even more difficult.

Rafael put his hand up and tipped it back and forth. "On the spectrum. She's only three, so..."

Alex rocked back on his heels. He knew that pause as well. The one that said, *Only time will tell and I wish like hell I had more of it. More for my kid and more for the work I love.* He would do anything in the world for Jake, but his love for medicine came a close second. Those two elements of his life had kept him from drowning in a world of pain after Amy's death. He saw it as his duty to make sure he gave each of them the respect and attention they deserved.

"I'd still be able to do the odd surgery at Boston Harbor?" Rafael looked in the direction of Boston, though they couldn't see it from here on the east side of the island.

"Absolutely. Cody and I both go over on a pretty regular basis, but prefer to live here."

"He's told me about his place and yours—"

"Yes, I've got the old farmhouse here on the clinic property."

"And what about Maggie?"

Alex nearly choked. Rafael had clearly heard Maggie's comment about the stir-fry after all but he feigned an air of nonchalance and pretended they were still talking about medicine. "Maggie Green? She's a physio, not a surgeon."

"Yes, of course. I met her at Boston Harbor. A real star in her field. I was actually asking something that probably isn't any of my business."

"What's that?" The way his heart pounded just that little bit faster every time he laid his eyes on her? Surely he hadn't been that obvious?

"You two are a couple, no?"

Alex gave a short, sharp laugh, "No! I mean, obviously she would be a lovely girlfriend for someone. Anyone, really. She's fantastic. Just..." *Dig. Dig. Dig.* "She's not *my* girlfriend."

Rafael gave him a sideways glance and shrugged the moment away. "Ah. My mistake. You just seemed to have..."

Sexual chemistry like there was no tomorrow?

"...a rapport."

A rapport.

The description pleased him. Alex had thought the constant back and forth between him and Maggie might have the potential to come across to patients as acrimonious, but...a rapport. He could live with that.

He thought of Maggie heading over to his house with his son. About as vivid a reminder a man could have that having her in his home meant developing both a rapport and a relationship. He slammed the mental door shut on that little nugget. Rapport was good for now. Relationship? Relationships were complicated and the last thing he needed was complicated.

CHAPTER NINE

"BUT, DAD, I promised Maggie we'd go and she's already been here *four whole days*!"

No one needed to tell Alex how long Maggie Green had been on the island. Their orderly, calm days had been up-ended by her daily delight in uncovering nooks and cran-nies of Maple Island he himself hadn't yet discovered.

And the clinic? The clinic had never seen such hurricane-force energy in one single human.

Her presence was being felt everywhere. Including right down in the core of his emotional epicenter. A very reluc-tant part of him was beginning to wonder if the missing element in his life was living in his spare room. And he wasn't entirely sure how he felt about it.

More time with Maggie meant yet more time acting like he barely noticed she was there. Acting wasn't his forte.

Jake's eyebrows were scrunched together in an increas-ingly familiar expression. This anxious, about-to-go-silent-for-hours-on-end face was usually caused by Alex's failure to understand the import of one thing or another. Or, as was often the case, simply not being there.

This time it was the request for his presence on a be-spoke "snacking tour" of downtown Maple Island. Such as it was.

There was Main Street. Half of the stores were shut for

"the season"—or lack thereof—and the harbor also had a smattering of stores and eateries, which she'd already seen.

"I'm not sure Maggie's interested in much beyond the stables. And her patients, of course."

At least, that was what he kept telling himself in order to stave off the idea that she might be trying to avoid him every bit as much as he'd been trying to avoid her. He even moved like one of Jake's toys. Stilted and awkward.

"I told her we'd go to Brady's."

"What for?"

"Duh. She's on the menu?" Jake shook his head, clearly astonished his father was so out of the loop.

"What? After four days?"

Jake nodded as if everyone on the island knew but her. "The Free Spirit Scramble." He grinned. "Maggie hasn't tried it yet so I promised her we would go."

I like it hot and spicy.

Unbelievable. She was already on the *menu*? He'd been here almost three years and— He tried to tamp down his indignation. Chances were high no one was craving a "Dr. Protocol" to start their day. Or to finish it, for that matter.

Tendrils of the man he used to be began reaching out and tickling his heart. He'd been a more carefree spirit once too. Sure, his upbringing had been tough, full of responsibilities a little boy shouldn't have to endure, but once he'd joined the military, he'd truly felt as if the world had been his oyster. He had been a man who could catch a woman's eye and hold it. A man who had married young, had had a son with the girl he'd thought he'd be with forever, only to lose her when he'd least expected it.

All the color had drained from his life on that day. And now he was just a bland scrambled eggs and a piece of toast without jam, rule-abiding, structure-loving know-it-all, who didn't know much of anything except for how to work and keep his son out of harm's way.

Maggie, who should've known better, was the polar opposite. She seemed intent on putting not only herself but everyone else she encountered right at the coalface. She'd nearly *lost her life* and seemed completely dedicated to squeezing every ounce of joy and color she could out of the rest of it.

Maybe...just maybe...it was time to take a leaf out of Maggie's book.

"Don't worry, Dad. We all know you work hard." Jake patted Alex's arm as though *he* were the father consoling the son for having tried hard but not quite making it up to the mark.

How could a seven-year-old boy make him feel like such a fuddy-duddy? Or was it the flame-haired, leggy, physiotherapist jogging toward them from the far end of the breezeway? And how did she make a jog seem like a slow-motion film sequence? All that hair flowing out behind her, creamy skin catching a hit of pink on her cheeks, lips parted just so....

"Da-a-a-d?" His son drew the word out into about fifteen syllables, each of them conveying a deepening level of frustration with his father.

Alex yanked his eyes away from Maggie and looked at his son. He could go for an all-day breakfast. It wasn't like it was a date or anything. He was a *military* man, for heaven's sake. He'd faced tougher enemies than a woman with a positive attitude and a body that—

A body that reminded him just how red-blooded a male he was.

He curtly reminded himself that Maggie was staff. An incredibly talented physiotherapist who brought a smile to the lips of just about everyone she met.

He blew out a short, sharp breath. He could do this. Absolutely. Even if she was unwittingly unearthing the fun guy buried somewhere underneath all the rules and regulations he'd taken to spouting whenever she was anywhere near him.

She was near them now. Her body still moving in that beautifully cadenced rhythm of hers. Her waist blooming out of the gentle curves of her hips, the arc and swoop of her breasts filling out the staff sweatshirt in way that made it look sexy. Sexy staff had been the last thing on his mind when he and Cody had bulk-ordered the clothes. Terrific. Yet another sensuality spanner Maggie had thrown into his perfectly ordered existence.

How *did* she run in slow motion?

"Da-a-a-d!"

"What's up, little man?" Maggie slowed to a stop in front of them, skin lightly glowing from the exertion. She gave Jake a quick high five before turning her bright smile on Alex. "So! Is it still all right to go into town? Not got any last-minute patients to see to?" The brightness in her eyes clouded ever so briefly as a hit of insecurity passed through them then disappeared as she turned her full-wattage grin toward Jake.

The muscles in Alex's jaw tensed as he ground his back teeth together. She'd obviously seen through his clever ploy to flee the house each night after they'd eaten supper together.

She'd obviously misconstrued his abrupt departures as disinterest rather than a man trying to avoid an increasingly unfettered attraction to a work colleague.

"Hey, Jakey? Do we think downtown Maple Island is ready to handle a bit of fun?" She raised her arms up as if she was at an all-night rave and knocked out a few gyrations that threw sparks straight into his erogenous zones.

For goodness' sake! They were with his *son*, not wandering round Boston's party zone!

Jake started dancing, too.

"Brady's does have a terrific soup and sandwich deal, which would be good for supper," Alex offered.

Jake turned to his father, appalled. "We're going to town to eat Maggie's all-day breakfast, *Dad*!"

"There's no rule that says you have to," Maggie said quietly, avoiding eye contact as she spoke.

That fierce protectiveness rose in him again. The one that not only couldn't bear the idea that he made Maggie feel uncomfortable, but the idea that someone else had frightened or hurt her in any way.

"No. You're right. There aren't." He took his car keys from his pocket and swung them in front of Jake and Maggie. "But sometimes rules—if they are to exist—are meant to be broken. Last one to the car is a rotten egg!"

He turned and took off running, a smile near enough splitting his face in two as Jake and Maggie stayed stationary, staring at him as if he'd just told them he was going to take up pole dancing.

"So. What do you think?" Fiona and Tom Brady had finally given up trying to casually stop by the booth Maggie, Alex and Jake were in and had plonked themselves down to get the lowdown.

"I think it's great." Maggie gave the pair a round of applause and nodded at Alex and Jake to do the same. Jake indulged her. Alex took a gulp of his coffee and lifted his eyebrows appreciatively.

It was hardly an over-the-top show of approval but...if she wasn't mistaken he was genuinely trying to be more relaxed around her. Make an effort. It made a nice change from the stiff formality, that was for sure. Jake seemed to bask in the glow of his father's goofier side. If you could call putting hot sauce on your hash browns in the shape of a smiley face goofy.

"Any tweaks? Any little changes?"

Maggie stared at her empty plate for a moment. "I like my hash browns extra crispy on the outside and all gooey hot inside." Her eyes traveled to Alex. Had she just described how she pictured him? She knew there was a fierce and loving heart beating inside that solid chest of his and yet he was certainly...crispy on the outside. She wondered whether or not his wife's death had taken away the gooey and hot inside.

"Well, that's all very achievable." Fiona pushed herself up and out of the booth and beckoned to her husband to join her. "Jakey? We're just about to make the night's last batch of crullers. Want to join us in the kitchen and then take a box home for the morning? We'll wrap him up in a double layer of aprons and a chef's jacket to make sure he's protected."

That last bit was obviously for Alex. His reputation for adhering to all codes of health and safety had clearly spread beyond the clinic's walls.

Jake's eyes went bright and he looked at his father expectantly. Maggie wished they'd invited her, too. What on earth was she going to talk with Alex about?

Patients.

Work was always good with him. Personal stuff? Not so much. Alex turned to her as if she had a say in the matter. "Sounds fun!"

For a split second it was as if they were a family. Her insides ached at how good it felt. Then ached again, knowing it was just a mirage. A blip of perfection in an otherwise imperfect world.

Alex made a hmm-haw noise, then caved. With conditions. Of course.

"Make sure you listen to everything Mr. and Mrs. Brady tell you. And don't eat all of the crullers before we get to the car!"

"Okay, Dad."

Alex ruffled his son's sandy blond hair and watched him follow the Bradys into the kitchen, that serious little face of his a mirror image of his father's.

The depth of love Maggie could see in Alex's eyes took her breath away. She ached to be near him. Touch him. Be

ANNIE O'NEIL

a part of the love he clearly felt for his son. A big enough
bombshell to make her jaw drop.

When he turned to look at her his eyebrows arched.

"What?" He swept a long-fingered hand across his face.
"I don't have any food on my face, do I?"

He didn't. But he wasn't to know that. So she reached
out and swept away a couple of invisible crumbs.

The connection was so strong when their eyes met she
forgot to breathe. When she dropped her hand from the
soft stubble lining his cheek, he caught her hand in his.

"What are we doing, Maggie?"

Oh, *crikey*. This hadn't been what she'd had in mind.
Had it? Or had she *wanted* this? Wanted to push at the invisible tension between them until it burst? But to what
end? Bring it to a halt or give it room to breathe and grow?

"Tell me," she said.

"What?" His eyebrows took a swan dive down toward
the center of his forehead.

"About your wife."

She felt just as surprised as Alex looked. And even more
surprisingly, he kept her hand in his and began to speak.

"Amy and I met in the military. First day of boot camp."
The shadow of a smile played upon his lips at the memory
and her heart leapt into her throat. She pressed her lips together and nodded. From the rasp in his voice as he carried
on speaking, he hadn't told this story much. And certainly
not to a woman with whom there was…whatever it was
that was going on between them.

A flirtation?

The beginnings of a romance?

One kiss didn't make it love, but…she was not immune
to this guy. Not by a long shot.

If only she felt brave enough. Secure enough. She felt
more sparks of attraction every time she looked at Alex, a
bonfire's worth of heat, but…she wasn't there yet. Maybe
she wouldn't ever be. But either way she wanted to be there

for him in this way. Listening. Understanding. Allowing
him to tell his story. To heal.

Maybe you could heal, too, if you told him what happened to you.

She forced herself to focus on Alex's beautiful green
eyes as he lightly touched on a childhood that had been less
than perfect, hence the early departure for the military. Arriving at boot camp and just hours later meeting his future
wife. She'd been cheering on all the men as they'd lined up
at the barber's for a buzz cut. He spoke of his wife's lonely
childhood. Their shared love of medicine. Hers for combat. His for...well, *after* combat. "Maybe that's why we
made such a good team." He let go of Maggie's hand and
sat back in the booth, shredding up a paper napkin as he
spoke. "She liked running into the firing line and I liked
pulling her out of it."

"Her very own knight in shining armor," Maggie whispered, then winced at Alex's pained expression.

"Something like that."

"Not that it sounded like she needed one," she quickly
recovered. She hadn't wanted a knight when she'd been
old enough to start thinking about love. Marriage. She'd
wanted someone to ride alongside. To complement her
rather than compensate for her.

Neither could she imagine Alex with anyone simpering
or weak. He had gone for a woman he'd met in the army.
His wife would have seen her ability to face fire as courage rather than foolhardiness.

That she understood.

She wondered if Alex did. Particularly when the consequences had been so extreme.

"She *did* need me," Alex ground out. "Just the one time.
The only time that mattered. And I wasn't there."

The bitterness swirled up into his throat as he spoke. He
blamed himself. Of course he did. As much as he would've

loved to squarely put the blame on Amy, rail against her inability to follow orders. She would be alive and well today if he'd been out there with her to pull her out of harm's way.

"What exactly happened?" Maggie's expression indicated he didn't have to tell her, but if he wanted to, she was there to listen. And for once he wanted to explain. Maybe she could help him understand whether he'd spent all these years angry with Amy or angry with himself.

He looked down at his hands and talked Maggie through the scenario. "She'd been working in one of the medical tents on the outskirts of a remote village in Afghanistan. One that had endured a lot of street combat and the residents had been the true victims. The medical tent was alerted to an incoming rocket-launched missile and, against orders, she stayed instead of evacuating."

"Why?"

"There were patients there who couldn't walk. She knew there wasn't time to move them all..." His guts twisted tightly at the memory. She'd given her life so that her patients hadn't died alone. Hadn't been abandoned.

"What an extraordinarily brave and generous thing to do." Maggie's hands flew to cover her mouth, but her eyes swam with unspilt tears. Tears of compassion.

He was just about to snap back that it wasn't very brave if you thought of the husband and child she'd left behind when it struck him. All these years he'd told himself Amy had chosen the patients over a life with him and Jake. That they hadn't been enough for her.

Sitting here, voicing his version of events to Maggie, he realized that's what it had been all along. A version. A crutch. A way for him to muddle through those first horrific weeks and months of loss, using anger as a fuel because it had seemed to be the only thing that had got him up and charged and able to proactively create the world for his son that he'd always wanted for him. The very same life he might be suffocating Jake with now. Life was full of risks. Even here on Maple Island. He was sure Old Salty could bend the ear of just about anyone who would listen until the cows came home about the perils of life in the clinic. The clinic!

He laughed.

"It's not funny!" Maggie looked appalled.

"No. No, it's not. I was just—" He felt his heart fill with gratitude that Maggie had come into his life. Made him look at things from another angle. Brought out his ability to laugh at life. At himself.

"I was just thinking about my reputation."

"What reputation? As a word-class rehab doctor?"

"More like as a world-class safety freak."

Maggie twisted her lips up into a tight dusty rose and then released them with a grin. "I wouldn't go so far as to call you a freak," she teased, before her expression sobered. "You know, maybe that's why Amy did what she did."

"What? Get herself killed?" He'd heard the bite in his voice. Maggie had too. He took a long draft of iced water as they let the moment pass.

"No." Maggie's voice was soft. "Risk her own life for someone else's. You said she was passionate about her duty as a soldier, didn't you?"

"Absolutely."

"Well...maybe she was doing what she thought you would. Protecting the people in her care."

And, just like that, all the anger and rage he'd felt about the injustice of his wife's early death dissipated.

She was absolutely right. He'd fight anyone and anything to protect the innocent.

Maybe his rage had been fueled by his own childhood. It wasn't as if he and Amy hadn't known the risks when they'd joined the military.

Early in his marriage he'd taken a phone call. A tough one. But it hadn't surprised him.

It had been from a police sergeant from his hometown.

A kid he'd grown up with who'd known him and his parents' reputation. They had both died in a drunk-driving car accident. Their old truck had flipped and ended up at the bottom of a ravine. As he'd listened to his former classmate go through the details, he'd felt a wash of emotions. Grief, of course. They had been his parents. But it had been a complicated grief. One colored with relief, sorrow, sadness for the childhood he'd never had and the loving relationship they could've shared if they'd stayed sober long enough to try.

His friend hadn't known it, but he'd just welcomed his son into the world. When he'd hung up the phone he'd vowed with every fiber in his being to provide his own family with as much stability as humanly possible. To give his son the childhood he'd never had.

He'd failed at the first hurdle.

In a moment of complete and open honesty he looked Maggie in the eye and said, "I lost a part of myself that day. The day the chaplain showed up at my door. I think I've been trying to figure out who or where on earth I am supposed to be ever since."

He half expected zany Maggie to surface and shout *Awkward!* But she didn't. She reached across the table, covered both of his hands with hers and said, "You are right here. Just where you're meant to be. It's okay to forgive yourself now. It's okay to be whoever you want to be. You've done everything right."

The power of her words surged straight into his heart with a healing warmth. A weight lifted off him that he hadn't even realized he'd been carrying. Guilt maybe? Anger.

Definitely.

Fear.

Probably a lot of that as well. Which was why Maggie and her free-spirited approach to life had no doubt rankled.

It didn't now.

It inspired. It lifted him up and out of that stagnant place he'd been sitting in emotionally for—well, for years now, he supposed. It was time to move on. With courage.

"Dad!" Jake burst out of the kitchen, carrying a tell-tale pink bakery box in his outstretched arms. "Look what I made!"

He laughed. Laughed for a dozen hand-made sticky sweet reasons. And he wasn't just talking about the mis-shaped crullers his son was already handing out to the handful of customers in the café. He laughed because his son had incredible timing when it came to interrupting intimate moments with Maggie. He laughed because he could suddenly think of his wife with a smile on his face. He laughed because he could. Maggie caught his eye and grinned before raising a cruller in a toast to him.

Here's to you, he thought as he accepted one of his son's gooey treats. He looked up and met Maggie's gaze again. *And here's to you, the woman who just might change my life.*

"Dr. Kirkland?" A man came around to their booth. "I thought that was you."

Maggie's blood ran cold at the sound of his voice. When their eyes met, it turned to ice.

"Hello, Eric."

At least he had the good grace to look uncomfortable.

The smile faded from Alex's lips when he caught the tension in the air. "I'm Dr. Kirkland, that's right. You two know each other?"

Maggie gave a quick, curt nod.

All the good feelings she'd been experiencing—the peace, the joy, the deep connection she felt with Alex—evaporated in an instant.

"Yeah!" Eric put out a fist for Maggie to bump, which she actively flinched away from. She wasn't going anywhere near that man. She tugged at the collar of her shirt, suddenly desperately needing some air.

Eric continued, slick as a snake oil salesman, "We knew each other back in the Boston Harbor Days until I went up a notch at a hospital out west."

Disbelief flooded her lungs and drowned out any retorts she could've made about what he'd actually done. Skipped town without so much as a fare-thee-well.

"Looking good, Mags. Got yourself a new job? Hobnobbing with the big boss man? Nice. I've heard great things about the clinic, Dr. Kirkland."

She watched as Jake, a naturally generous kid, looked at his crullers, looked at Maggie, then Eric and firmly closed the lid of the box.

His innate sense that something wasn't right tugged at her heart, which was quite a feat considering that very same heart was ricocheting round her chest like a caged she-devil.

She didn't dare look at Alex. This man standing in front of them, so cavalier, had made her feel smaller than anyone had in her entire life. Had ground her sense of confidence to dust. It had literally taken her years to get to this place again. The one where she could be confident. Strong.

Eric cleared his throat and pushed himself up to his full height and started explaining why he was back in town. Catching up with friends at Boston Harbor. He was over on the island with a friend he pointed out. They were "checking out the scene."

The whole time he spoke Maggie wished she could curl up into a tiny ball and roll away. Mortification didn't begin to cover it.

She'd been bowled over by this man. His good looks. His ability to charm. Talk a good game. Now she saw all his alpha behavior for what it really was. Slick, superficial power plays to cover up an utterly hollow interior. The man had the emotional depth of a toad.

No. That was being mean to toads. They could turn into princes.

Princes were good and kind. At least the fairy-tale variety were.

Her gaze flicked to Alex and at precisely that moment his eyes met hers and they held tight. She saw the flash of understanding light then take fire. His shoulders broadened. He gave his son's arm a squeeze then turned his attention on Eric, his voice deep and solid. "If you'll excuse us, we've got to get this little guy home."

"Oh, right." Eric stared at Alex and Maggie. His eyes dropped to their fingers. For some inexplicable reason Maggie quickly hid her hands so he couldn't tell whether she was married to Alex or not. At this particular minute she wished she was. A lot. Alex Kirkland was a true man. A gentleman. She could— *Oh, wow.* She could grow to trust Alex Kirkland.

"You lot off back home?" Fiona Brady bustled up to the table with another pink box and handed it over to Maggie. "Thought you might like these for the morning." She winked then shot a saucy look at Alex. "Something to keep a smile on yer fella's face."

What? Fiona knew as well as anyone on Maple Island that Alex Kirkland was a committed widower and— more importantly—a father. He wouldn't... Wait a minute. Was she joining in the ruse to confuse Eric? Were they all banding together because they'd seen her discomfort? She scanned the café and saw Tom Brady flicking the sign on the front door from Open to Closed. Eric saw it, too.

"We were just going to order," he protested.

"Sorry, pal." Tom shrugged as if he didn't have a care in the world then folded his arms across his meaty chest. "Closing early tonight. Bad luck."

A bolt of energy shot through her.

They were all joining together to help her.

Jake, Tom, Fiona. Alex. She even saw a couple of the

staff from behind the counter square their shoulders as the tension grew. Extraordinary. They were giving her a support system without even knowing what Eric had done to her. This was what a community did for one another. The power of that realization surged through her with the same rush of adrenaline she'd felt when she'd won gold. Or taken her first steps with her first set of prosthetics. When she'd known she would live.

She turned to Eric, gave him a quick up and down scan. He wasn't all that. "Goodnight."

Then she turned and walked out the door Tom was holding open, with Jake and Alex following in her wake.

When they got into the car she was shaking like a jelly.

They rode home in silence and after Jake had been safely tucked up in bed Alex came downstairs and sat on the sofa where Maggie had been trying to process what had happened.

She was safe here. Secure. But she still didn't know how to rein in that painful feeling of shame Eric had unleashed in her back then.

He'd said he couldn't be with her. This after he'd told her she was beautiful. Beautiful until he'd seen her legs. Seen who she really was without the high heels. Without the horse-riding boots. With nothing on but herself.

And he'd told her the only thing that would allow him to be with her was pity.

Her stomach churned at the memory.

"Want to talk about it?" Alex's voice was soft. Concerned.

"Not particularly." She knew she should be garnering strength from him, from the show of community solidarity, and yet... She wasn't there yet.

"Would you like to go up to your room?"

She nodded. Yes. Yes, she would. And then she'd like to knot together all the sheets and climb out of the win-

dow and run far, far away to a place where all her emotions
didn't collide with the past in such a painful way.

She looked at Alex who had his own past to deal with.
His own pain. His own hurdles to leap. And then it hit her.
Her past lived deep within her. She was the only one who
had the power to let it surge up and overwhelm her, or...
to simply own it...and move on. There wasn't anywhere in
the world she could escape it. Nowhere was safe.

And just like that, Alex pulled her into his arms and
was kissing her.

You're safe in his arms.

A battle began between her heart and her mind. Nowhere was safe until she made peace with her past. With
the cruel things Eric had said.

Her body was responding to Alex's. To his touch. The
heat that flared between them each time their lips met.

As much as she wanted it—as much as she wanted
him—tonight was not the night to do this.

As gently as she could, she pulled away. She ran her fingers along his stubbled cheeks, tipped her forehead to his.

"Are you okay?"

She shook her head. "Not really. But I will be."

He nodded. "It's been a bit of a crazy night."

"You've got that right." She reached out and stroked his
cheek again. He'd been so open with her. So honest. She
wanted to do the same for him, but...

The tiniest shoot of belief that one day she might be
able to blossomed as he dropped a kiss on her forehead.

"I don't know what's happening between us. But how
about we admit that it's *something*?"

"Yes," she said. "It is something. I'm just not sure I
know how to take the next step."

He shrugged, opened his hands up to the heavens. "For
once, we are on the same page."

They laughed, the connection between them deepening

with the acknowledgement that whatever it was between them deserved recognition. Time.

Space.

"I think I'm going to tackle those stairs now." Her knees were miles better and doing something under her own steam was the only way she was going to come to terms with what had happened with Eric.

"I'm just going to catch up on some paperwork." Alex didn't move from the sofa as she rose.

"Need me to bring your helmet down?"

He laughed. "Not tonight. Tonight I think I'll be all right."

She had to stop herself from blowing him a kiss. She felt so damn close to the man and yet...

"Night-night."

"Night, Maggie. Sweet dreams."

After she was cozily tucked into bed she knew she was going to have to wage a war. She deserved to be happy. Alex deserved it too. Neither of them should be in this bonkers holding pattern. They either had to go for it and explore what was happening between them, or simply admit she couldn't find a way to overcome the shame and insecurity she'd been carrying with her these three long years.

She rolled over and let her pillow drown out her scream of frustration.

If she didn't? She'd be stuck in a cycle of possibility and pain forever.

CHAPTER TEN

"Got a hackamore I can use?" Maggie ran her hand along the warmth just below the mare's mane.

Randy gave a low whistle of approval. "Instead of a proper bridle? You up to it?"

She nodded. She wasn't one to pull out her steamer trunk full of trophies, ribbons and medals to prove a point and Randy had yet to connect the dots.

They popped the bit-less bridle onto the horse and while Randy wandered off to find something else, Maggie tried something she hadn't in a while. Mounting a bareback horse without a leg up.

"There's a good girl. Good girl." She took a big fistful of mane in her left hand, then with a quick one-two hop, jump and a cinch on Skylla's withers... *Aha!*

"Here we are— Oh." Randy appeared round the corner with a mounting block in one hand and a saddle on his arm.

"Oops." Maggie grinned down at him from atop the horse. "I shoulda said."

"Yeah," Randy said dryly. "Maybe you coulda given me a bit of a heads-up that you were a circus performer in a past life."

She laughed. She'd actually always wanted to be in the circus. Had planned to run away and do all sorts of tricks on the back of her pony. Her mother would've murdered her if she'd known just how many handstands she'd done on her pony's bare back before she'd gotten sick. After that? She'd tried twice as hard. "I've got safety harnesses if you got any other tricks up your sleeve." He pointed to a couple of ropes hanging from one of the rafters, proving it took one daredevil to know another.

"When you get back from your ride, make sure you stop by the tack room," Randy continued. "There might be something in there that would interest you."

"Will do." She tipped her invisible hat to him, clicked to the horse and gave her a light nudge with her heels, smiling as Randy gave her a quick farewell salute. She liked bantering with him. The kind where you could throw insults that didn't stick back and forth at each other. Her parents had done that loads and had told her trainers when she'd started on dressage to do the same. "Treat her exactly the same as you would anyone," they'd said. "Exactly the same."

Which everyone had always done, except Eric.

That sour twist of shame threatened to swirl up and tighten her throat, draining her lungs of air, but she fought it this time. For a week and a half, ever since that day at the bakery, she'd been shoving it down and shoving it down, and it looked like today was the day she couldn't rein it in anymore.

And why should she? She was a woman who could command a sixteen-hand horse with a little flick of her wrist. A nudge with her heel. The strength of her attitude.

Why had she allowed Eric to make her feel so small?

It suddenly seemed insane she had let him have any power over her in the first place. Even an iota. Anyone who thought they were doing a person a kindness by telling them they would be a "pity lay" was a certifiable jackass.

The coarseness of his language shuddered down her spine so powerfully she practically felt it shoot out the soles of her boots.

She pressed her eyes tight and pictured exactly that. The cruel words, the hurt feelings, the sour taste—all of it—

just flowed out of her boots and into the sawdust and into a big old pile of horse manure. Right where it belonged.

A rush of strength washed through her like pure oxygen. She needed to get out of the barn. Remind herself of the woman she knew she really was. Fierce. Loyal. Strong. *Sensual*. Able to love and be loved. That's who she was. Not this weird happy-one-minute-scaredy-pants-the-next victim. No. She'd never let anyone make her feel small ever again.

Randy called out as she turned Skylla toward the big barn doors. "It's cold as all get-out. You're more than welcome to ride in the covered ring if you like."

"Nope. I'm good." She beamed. "I could do with knocking a few more cobwebs loose."

Eric-shaped cobwebs. And maybe then she'd have a clear enough head to figure out what the heck was happening between her and Alex. Enjoy a few more of those kisses. And perhaps a bit more.

The cold air hit her fast and hard when she and Skylla turned the corner toward the path leading to the waterfront. She could practically feel her smile hitting each of her ears. She dug her heels into Skylla's sides. Time to get both of their hearts pumping with a good old-fashioned gallop.

Out of the corner of his eye, Alex saw Maggie heading from the stables on a huge mare out toward the coastal path. Ever since the bakery outing, she'd practically been living in the stables.

He shouldn't have kissed her. Not when she'd so clearly been upset.

He pocketed his tablet, gave a final note about changing Salty's medication to the nurse, instantly experiencing a sting of loss when he realized he'd missed that last glimpse of Maggie as she and the horse had disappeared around the corner.

Exactly the same niggle that had been gnawing at his conscience reared its head again.

That man had done something awful to Maggie. He'd had to hold himself in tightly not to pull him off his feet, push him up against a wall of the bakery and demand the truth.

But it was Maggie's story to tell. Maggie's truth to manage. All of which landed him straight back at the place he'd been fastidiously trying to avoid.

It was time to get some appropriate accommodation organized for her. Not only was having her in his home impractical, it was…distracting. When you looked at the situation square in the eye, they were living together. And…he liked it. It worked. She made his son laugh. Her French toast was the best he'd ever tasted. She loved his spaghetti—his signature dish. Or at least was good at faking it.

Day by day she was becoming part of his family's fabric and for the first time in six years he thought he could see the possibilities of that happening. The thoughts tugged him toward the daycare center where Jake was at the after-school club.

But if she didn't feel she could trust him enough to tell him what had happened to make her pull back? It wasn't a fabric that could hold.

Give her time.

He walked into the daycare center and right away he picked his son out from the smattering of children and gave Jake a wave.

His son didn't notice. He was utterly engrossed in making one of his Christmas presents. A huge construction project that Maggie had helped him bring over in the morning after they'd tried and failed to put it together the night before. Alex had been relatively certain the "failure" had come about because Maggie had kept taking pieces and using them as comedy eyebrows or miniature beards on herself, trying to make Jake laugh. It had worked. But when she'd seen Alex watching them, all the spark had drained from her eyes.

He was trying not to take it personally. She'd only developed that vacant expression since the run-in with that man at the bakery. Another part of him wanted to pull his heart out of his chest and say, *Here! I've shown you mine. Show me yours!* And the other part of him just wanted his calm, quiet, life back.

He watched his son. Now that Jake was able to concentrate properly, the structure was taking shape. A brick by brick towering beast of a Tyrannosaurus rex.

He scanned the other after-school daycare kids. One pair was playing a ferocious game with swords. Another pair was pretending they were lions or tigers, judging by the roars coming from their corner. And yet another pair was playing a board game that had them in gales of laughter.

His child was the only one on his own.

Jake had never really struck him as a loner but... Alex scratched his jaw thoughtfully. He'd always been a serious little boy and lately he was beginning to question just how much that had to do with him.

The joy on Jake's face when he'd bumped down the stairs with Maggie that first night...it had felt like lighting up the Empire State Building right inside his heart. Ditto to the arm-wrestling championship she'd organized, the lesson on how to make pancakes with smiley faces on them...

Maggie had burst into their lives like a field of tulips coming to bloom in a single moment—he'd felt alive again. Yet this past couple of weeks, when she'd pulled right back just as he'd been ready to start taking steps forward?

He'd let himself fall back into his old reserved habits to protect himself, but this time the "Mr. Protocol" suit wasn't fitting well at all. It was too tight. Restrictive. He wanted to live again, not watch life pass him by.

Frustration crackled through him. And he had one very

flame-haired, brown-eyed, feisty-spirited idea why he was suddenly questioning the way he lived his life.

"That is a pretty serious model he's got going on."

Alex had been so deep in thought he started at the sound of Summer's voice.

"Jake's been at it since he arrived." The daycare worker smiled warmly. "It always fascinates me to see a child so engrossed in something and your boy has concentration down to a T! I think he's refused three games of tag and one offer of a piggy-back ride so he can keep on working."

Like father, like son.

Maggie had asked him if he'd wanted to join her and Jake play board games for the past couple of nights, but he'd begged off. Paperwork, he'd said. It hadn't been paperwork at all.

It had been that urge to kiss her, taste her, slip his hands against her bare skin that had kept him holed up in his office late at night as she and Jake had giggled away until he'd stomped down the stairs, back stiff from using the wrong chair at his desk, and announced it was bedtime.

Truth was, he wanted a relationship with her. And this whole "giving her time" thing was gnawing away at his sanity.

Summer shifted her gaze to Alex. "Everything all right?"

"Yes. Absolutely." He forced himself to smile back. "You're new here, right?"

"Yes, sir."

"Alex. Please call me Alex. I was just wondering, from a newcomer's perspective, does Jake strike you as being *too* serious?"

Summer looked up to the right, a common tell that she was giving the matter proper consideration.

"I think every child is different. And what you and Cody have created here... This place..." She opened her arms and scanned the warmly lit and comfortably furnished room. "It's so much more than a daycare center. I actually call it an imagination castle. It's got everything that will bring out the best in them. Whether they're an intro- vert, an extrovert, a scientist, a builder—" She laughed as one of the little boys "died" after the other boy plunged his sword between the other's arm and stomach. "What- ever they want. They know they are being cared for. They know the people who love them most are nearby. They know they're safe."

Alex's shoulders relaxed a bit. The magic word. "Safe."

"Right! Good. Well, I guess I better get back to work, then." He waved at Jake again. He looked up this time and smiled, waved back. Alex's heart thumped against his rib- cage. He loved that little boy to within an inch of his own life. More. But he worried every day that the life he was giving him was maybe...a bit too safe?

Perhaps now was the time to push his own boundaries. Experience what it felt like to not just dip his toe back into the land of the living but to dive in head first.

A couple of hours later than he'd hoped, Alex went back to the daycare center to collect Jake. Only when he scanned the sea of little boys' and girls' heads...his son's wasn't there.

Panic pierced through him like shrapnel.

"Jake? Jakey! Summer? Where's Jake?"

Summer jogged up to him, her brow furrowed with con- fusion. "Didn't Maggie say? She came by an hour or so earlier. She said she had a surprise or something for him down at the barns. I thought you knew."

An irrational fear gripped his heart. She was letting his son ride but he didn't know how to. He'd seen her ride off without a helmet. She took risks.

Summer's brow furrowed. "I'm sorry, Dr. Kirkland, I just presumed—"

"Don't ever, *ever* presume when it comes to Jake."

Summer paled at the admonishment. "I'm so sorry. Jake

was so happy to see her it seemed almost as though they had planned it."

Alex swallowed and tried not to let the swell of rage and fear he was feeling lash out at Summer. "Not your fault. I'm sure everything's fine."

"I should have called," Summer said to his back as he turned to leave.

"Yes," he said under his breath as he pushed through the door and began to run to the barns. "You should have."

Moments later, the roar of blood pounding through his head, he was pulling open the barn doors. Jake was sitting on a saddle stand, applauding.

The relief he felt turned to instant anger when he saw what—or rather, who—Jake was applauding.

Maggie was doing a handstand on a moving horse.

No helmet. No straps.

She was holding onto some sort of bar mounted on the horse's shoulders, but apart from that? She was about three seconds away from a fall that could break her neck and kill her.

Fury roared through him. How dared she risk her life that way? And right in front of his son. A kid who was obviously falling in love with her. A kid who had lost his mother. No way in hell was he going to let his child experience that type of loss again.

Maggie lowered herself onto the horse's back and froze when she saw Alex striding toward her. He did not look happy.

"What the hell do you think you're doing?"

Wow. Definitely not happy. She flicked her eyes toward Jake. "I'm just showing your son some of my repertoire."

"Without a helmet?" His voice was low and white hot with rage. "Was that clever? Doing such a dangerous act in front of a child?"

"It's okay, Daddy." Jake slid off the saddle stand, ran up

and took his father's hand in his. "I'm fine. Maggie was showing me her tricks."

She held up her hands. "I'm sorry. I know I'm not wearing a helmet, but look—" She reached round to her back and unclipped the safety wire. She showed him the clip. "See? I was clipped in the whole time."

"Maggie clipped me in, too, so it was safe," Jake said, tugging on his father's hand.

Alex's voice dropped another notch. "What do you mean, she clipped you in, too?"

"When I was doing handstands."

Everything about him stilled. The only thing Maggie could see moving on Alex was the carotid artery at the base of his neck thumping so hard she knew exactly which way his blood pressure was going.

This had been a very bad idea.

Alex dropped down on one knee, cupping his son's small shoulders in his large surgeon's hands. "Jakey, can you run on home now? We'll get something together for supper in a little while, but I need to have a word with Maggie first."

"But we had a surprise for you."

"You can give it to me later, son."

Jake sent a pleading look toward Maggie. He didn't want to go. She didn't want him to either.

"Jake." Alex tipped his head toward the barn doors. "You go on home now, please."

Her lungs ached from holding her breath.

Randy appeared from nowhere. "Want me to take the horse and stable her up?"

Maggie nodded, her hands shaking as she handed him the reins. "Thanks for finding me the vaulting roller."

"My pleasure, Miss Maggie." He tipped his cowboy hat and shot a look at Alex. "I'll leave you to it."

This was bad. This was really, really bad.

He wasn't shouting. His face wasn't puce. He wasn't looming over her in a threatening way. But that *stillness*...

When they were left on their own Alex finally met her eye and said quietly, "Would you mind explaining to me what on earth possessed you to risk my son's life in that way?"

"There was no risk. I was only teaching him hand-stands—"

"On a moving horse? You know he's never ridden, don't you?"

Intellectually, she knew where this was coming from. Alex liked to dot his I's and cross his T's. She should've checked with him beforehand.

Emotionally? She felt backed up against a wall and there was no way she was going to let him steamroller her into admitting she'd done something reckless when she hadn't.

"When we did it with Jake, we were completely sta-tionary."

"We? Who's 'we'?"

She was fighting mad now. How dared he not trust her with Jake? He wasn't the only one who had feelings for the little boy. "Randy was here. I was holding Jake the en-tire time. The horse was tied to a hitching post. Jake was clipped into the safety harness. There wasn't a single un-safe thing about it." She jabbed a finger into that hard chest of his, refusing to yelp when she felt it jam against the wall of muscle there. "So, if I were you, instead of marching in here and being all King Kong about everything, I would take a step back and cool your jets, pal."

He took a step back.

But from the daggers he was throwing her from his eyes, she knew she shouldn't have told him to cool his jets.

She didn't have any family left.

Didn't have a child.

Didn't know the pain of sudden tragic loss in the way Alex did.

And she'd made him relive his biggest fear. Losing his son.

He opened his mouth, pointed at her furiously—then shook his head, turned on his heel and walked away.

CHAPTER ELEVEN

IT TOOK ALL her courage to go back to the house.

She'd waited, of course, for him to calm down. Had helped Randy groom horses who were already glistening until she had no choice but to leave the barns.

Never before had her feet felt like cement blocks as she walked up the ramp to Alex's porch.

For the first time since she'd arrived, she knocked on the front door, reminding herself that just as he'd tapped into her fear of physical intimacy, she'd tapped into his today. Loss.

She forced her shoulders down from her ears and waited.

He opened the door but didn't say anything. He didn't need to.

"May I come in?"

He looked over his shoulder back into the house and called out, "Head on up to your room, bud. I'll be with you in a minute."

She saw Jake run up the stairs. When he got to the top he turned and gave her a timorous wave followed by a good-luck pair of thumbs-up.

Her heart pounded against her chest so hard she thought it was going to explode.

When her eyes dropped back to meet Alex's, he stepped to the side and let her in.

This felt awful.

Crazy awful.

And then the apologies began pouring out.

"Okay. First of all, let me apologize. I should have told you I was picking him up from daycare, presuming it would be all right with you. It will not happen again. Not without your express permission."

A muscle in his jaw twitched. Alex was most likely resisting telling her she wouldn't be getting his permission for anything beyond doing her job and that better be done to the letter or else she may as well not even bother seeing out her contract.

"Secondly?" She flicked her thumb up toward Jake's room. "I love that little boy. There isn't a single, solitary thing on this earth I would do to compromise his welfare. Not a thing. I promise you with all my heart we did everything in our power to keep him safe."

The irritation she'd seen crackle through his eyes diminished. A little.

"I don't understand why you did it at all."

"We—he wanted to surprise you."

"What? By doing a trick where he could break his—?" He stopped himself, held up his hands. "I don't know, Maggie. There seems to be something more going on here. You won't talk to me. You don't want..." he moved his hand between them "...whatever this is going on with us."

"That's not true! That's not true at all!"

She did want a relationship with him. She was just scared. Too scared.

"Then why won't you talk to me?"

"How can I when you go berserk over something that wasn't even a problem?"

Okay, that wasn't strictly fair, but she was caught up in the moment too. Fighting for—she wasn't entirely sure what she was fighting for. Her right to be heard?

He sucked in a deep breath. The kind that told her he was going to explain to her exactly how she could talk to him. What came out instead was a sigh. A sad sigh. He raked his hand through his hair and looked up at the ceiling. Finally he looked at her again.

"So, you're saying that by bursting into the barn like a he-man, I ruined my son's big surprise."

Maggie scrunched her features up tight and pinched her fingers together. "A little bit."

"A lotta bit, from the sound of things." He huffed out a sigh and dropped into a deep-seated armchair. "I don't seem to be getting much right these days."

The hairs went up on Maggie's arms. Oh, no. This wasn't the way the conversation was meant to go. She was the one who should be bearing the brunt of the *mea culpas*.

"That's complete malarkey."

Much to her surprise, Alex laughed. "Malarkey, is it?"

She replied, stone-cold serious. "Absolutely. Alex, please let me apologize again. From the bottom of my heart. I never meant to scare you like that. I thought it would be okay, but I obviously should've asked you first."

Alex gave a little nod. One that just might, if she were squinting, allow for a teensy bit of leeway when it came to any future surprises she or Jake might plan to give him.

"Look…" she brandished her finger "…you built this whole entire place for your son, right?"

He tipped his head back and forth as if trying to slot the words into the right position. "That was definitely one of the reasons, yes."

"As a tribute to your wife and, obviously, an unbelievably amazing place for your patients as well. But when I spoke with Cody during my interview I got the sense that the two of you really wanted to build this place so you could get your work-life balance straight. Make sure your children had the best care possible while you were at work. When you boil it down? All of this is for Jake. So, when there's even a *suggestion* that there are any holes in your plan, you go a bit bonkers. Or did I get that wrong, too?"

"No." He shot her a sidelong look with those beautiful green eyes of his. "You're right."

She stopped herself from giving a little victory punch into the air, wove her fingers together and forced herself to sit on the sofa across from him and rest them in her lap instead. Listening was every bit as powerful as being right. Now was a time to listen.

Alex gave her one of those professorial looks of his that she was beginning to find incredibly endearing. They weren't as judgmental as she'd originally thought. They were his way of buying time while he considered what to say or do.

She waited patiently, trying her best not to think about what it would feel like if she crossed to him, ran her fingers through his hair and tipped his head back so she could give him a deep, consoling, loving kiss.

Uh...hold your horses and tighten the reins!

Loving?

Okay. It wasn't like she was *in* love with the man. Sure, she thought he was an incredible doctor. Plus he smelled amazing. Kissed like a freaking Greek god... His hands were also pretty nice. Especially when they were on her bum.

She glanced at them.

Okay, it had only been the once, but it had felt great and his hands weren't just nice—they were actually spectacular. All big and strong and male.

But loving? The completely natural thought suggested her feelings were taking a journey she had very specifically forbidden them to take.

One glance told her all she needed to know. His kind face. The crinkles by his eyes she would've sworn had come from laughter. And concern. His ability to nurture. That *hair*. Those *lips* of his. Ridiculous. Ridiculously off limits more like.

And she was falling head over heels in love with him.

Alex opened his palms in an apologetic gesture. "I shouldn't have jumped to imagining the worst-case scenario. I should've trusted that you had Jake's best interests at heart."

His words arrowed straight into her heart and pounded through her veins.

Trust.

It was something she valued beyond anything. Well, on a par with respect. Trust and respect. Without those two things?

You couldn't have love.

She let her hands drop to her sides and looked him straight in the eye. "I'll admit I spent a lot of time sitting under a pretty dark cloud before I built up my 'silver linings' skills. I got sick when I was thirteen. That's given me eighteen years of practice. You've only had, what? Six at best? Total novice. It'll come. The fact you responded as you did is a credit to you. To the love you have for your son. My parents' love for me was just as fierce and let me tell you it gave me the strength to become who I am today. Even if I am a little bit of a loony sometimes."

There was more to it. Of course there was. She just didn't know how to tell him. Or even *if* she should tell him. Would he even be interested?

Alex swiped a hand across his face and sat forward in his chair. "I'm sorry I came blasting into the barn like an insane poppa bear."

"And I'm sorry I gave you cause to. I think I went a bit 'Goldilocks' on you and your family."

He let his smile broaden. "I did invite you to stay here."

"But maybe I've made myself a bit too much at home?"

Alex gave his jaw a scrub.

The silence was unbearable.

Oh, God. She was going to have to move out. Right now. This minute. He didn't want her here anymore.

He pointed up the stairs. "I've got a reading date with

a little boy right now. Help yourself to some supper from
the kitchen, and maybe we should talk about this again
afterwards."

As soon as he disappeared up the stairs Maggie dropped
her head into her hands. She'd ruined everything. She'd
stay here tonight because she had nowhere else to go, but
in the morning? In the morning she'd hand in her notice.

Was it cowardly?

Of course it was.

But could she bear living a separate life from the two
people she now considered the closest thing to family she
would ever let herself have?

Not for a New York second.

"Dad!" Jake gave his dad's arm a poke with one of his
little-boy fingers. "You've already read that part. *Three*
times." He heaved out a dramatic sigh.

Maybe if he stopped thinking about Maggie and how
to convince her to stay, he'd be better at this.

He stared at the page. Couldn't even remember where
he'd left off.

"Enough for tonight?"

"If you're going to keep reading the same paragraph
over and over I might as well do it myself." He scrunched
up his face. There was obviously more.

"What?"

"You don't do it like Maggie does."

This caught his attention.

"Maggie's read to you?"

His son gave him a look as if he'd lost a few brain cells
on the walk back home from work. "Didn't you notice?"

"What?"

"That for the last week or so we've started about twenty
pages further on from when we stopped the night before."

"When did she read to you?"

"Sometimes she brings my book into the daycare center. When I go there after school."

The knot of emotions tangled up in his chest doubled
in size. What was he feeling? Jealousy? Relief? Hope that
maybe he'd found someone who could genuinely love both
him and his son?

Careful, you're a long way from that, pal.

Jake rearranged himself so he was staring at the book and
not his father as he continued quietly, "She does great character voices. Maybe if you were a bit nicer to her then she
would stay longer than three months and teach you how
to do them too."

All the breath left Alex's lungs.

Wow.

"Would you like that? If Maggie stayed?"

Alex didn't know if he wanted to hear the answer. His
heart was twisted so tightly inside his ribcage he could
hardly breathe.

The clinic made huge demands on his time and even he
had to admit he didn't always get the balance right.

Jake was enjoying having a woman around the house.
No, it was more than that. He was enjoying having *Maggie* round the house. She was fun. She saw the bright side
of life, even when she was clearly distracted. Sure, he'd
near enough ripped her head off when his fear over his
son's safety had morphed into rage, but once he'd cooled
down, listened to her, it was obvious she had been acting
totally responsibly.

I love that little boy.

It was a huge admission. Enormous from someone who
was still bottling up a secret and keeping him at arm's
length, both physically and emotionally.

Was that the real reason why he had been so angry with
her? Because he'd invested all this trust in her and she still
didn't trust him?

Well, what do you know? Instead of making him want to run like hell, he'd realized the war that had been raging inside him since the first time he'd laid eyes on her had been because he wanted her to stay, too. And for a whole lot of different reasons than his son did.

"She's nice," Jake said, still not meeting his father's gaze.

Alex put his arm round his son and pulled him close. "That she is, Jakey, boy. That she is."

After tucking him in, he walked to the next room and saw Maggie's bedroom light was on. She must have decided she didn't want to talk about it anymore. He knocked softly, not entirely sure what he was going to say.

"Yes?"

He opened the door and almost shut it again. Maggie was sitting on the bed, bathed in the warm glow of the bedside lamp. She wasn't wearing her prosthetics and was tugging a blanket over her legs. Not quickly enough for him to miss a glimpse of her thighs, her short pajama bottoms hugging the curves of her derriere and a figure-hugging tank top. He gripped the door handle until his knuckles turned white.

He definitely wanted her to stay.

"Yes?" she asked again, her eyebrows crinkling at his muteness. She arranged the blanket a little more tightly over her knees.

He threw his planned speech out the window and ad-libbed. "I just wanted to say thanks. For the surprise."

She barked a short laugh. "Yeah. I don't think I'll be pulling off any more coups like that anytime soon."

"No. Seriously. I overreacted. I should've trusted you."

He watched her process the honest apology and was honored to see it finally hit home. She valued trust every bit as much as he did.

Their gazes met. Heat flared in his chest bright and hot. He knew right then and there that he wanted more than this. More than different bedrooms. More than stumbling over awkward apologies for fights they never should have had. He wanted her. He wanted Maggie.

He came into the room, leant down, cupped her face in his hands and kissed her lips more softly than he'd kissed anyone.

She pulled back but in such a way that their lips brushed against the other's all over again. It was intoxicating.

"I think I'd better get to sleep," she whispered. "It's been a long day."

Her fingertips pressed against her lips as he rose up to his full height. She'd felt it, too. He could see it in the high shine of her dark eyes.

"Well, goodnight, then," she said.

He knew a cue to leave when he heard one. But her eyes told a different story.

She wanted him as much as he wanted her.

Leaving would be the sensible thing to do. The *practical* thing. But for the first time in over half a dozen years he wished like hell he hadn't folded himself into the narrow confines of a man who played his whole life by the rulebook.

So he threw that out the window, too.

"What happened?"

"When? Today? I told you—"

"No. Not with the horseback handstands. With that man. The one at the Bradys' bakery."

Her brown eyes turned pitch black. "That's not a very nice story."

"Is it one I ought to hear?"

She knew what he was asking. He wanted her and if anything was going to happen between them, they needed complete and total honesty between them.

She stared at him for a moment, her expression completely neutral...and then crossed her arms tightly in front of her as if protecting herself in advance of whatever his reaction might be.

He sat at the end of the bed.

"You sure you want to hear this?"

"Absolutely."

Three years' worth of tension and pain worked itself free and flowed like hot lava through her veins.

Alex wanted to hear her story.

He cared.

He trusted her.

She knew now the love she thought she might feel for him was genuine and true. So she forced herself to bare her emotional scars to him just as he had for her. She may as well go physical, too. She moved the blanket away so that her legs were fully exposed below the knee.

Alex didn't bat an eyelid.

So she started talking.

"We dated."

Alex pulled his knee up and tucked it under his other leg. "Right. This was back in Boston?" He was fact-gathering. Not judging. She filled her lungs with a deep breath of courage and continued.

"We met through a friend. Another physio I worked with. We dated for a while with the proviso—my proviso—that we take things slow. He…" Her eyes shifted up to the ceiling to pick the best description, then looked back down to meet Alex's steady, warm, gaze. "Let's just say the man could sell ice to penguins. He had the gift of the gab and was on a dedicated charm offensive. I'd never been so actively…wooed, I guess. He really went for it. Called me all the time. Texted. Sent flowers. He told me I was beautiful, smart, talented, and I totally bought it. Hook, line and sinker."

"All of those things are true, though," Alex said.

Heat crept into her cheeks and she batted away the compliment. She needed to get through this. "Anyway. I had dated a couple of people before. People in the equestrian scene. People with…" She blew out a breath to stave off the sting of tears. "People like me." She pointed to her legs, though she didn't need to. "So it wasn't as if I hadn't had experience with the physical side of things, but Eric was the first so-called able-bodied man I'd ever been with."

Now that she could see the situation clearly, she saw how over the top he'd been with her. How she'd been some sort of special notch to his bow. The Paralympian with a hot body and flame-colored hair. The papers had billed her as a modern-day Aphrodite. A symbol to all women who wanted to soar up and surpass all expectations. A golden girl. And it still hadn't been enough for him.

Alex reached out and gave her leg a squeeze. The gesture sent a thousand rays of reassurance through her. "There's no need to hash over all of the details, but suffice it to say I took my time letting things get physical between us. And when they finally went beyond kissing…"

Alex drew in a sharp breath, one that seemed to know what was coming. So she cut to the chase. "Once he saw me without my prosthetics, he looked horrified. I don't know what he'd expected to see. He knew my feet were all made for me. Too real looking, I guess." She had to laugh, though there was nothing funny about what had happened. "Fooled him until the very last hurdle. When I took them off, he was clearly repelled by the reality. Said he just couldn't. That if he were to have sex with me it would be out of pity. Pity!"

The word burned her throat as she spoke it and hot tears of fury she'd never let free flowed down her cheeks. In an instant Alex was beside her, pulling her into his arms, holding her tightly to him as she released the rest of the rage and anger that someone had ever made her feel so much shame. She'd given Eric that power. And from this moment on she was taking it back.

CHAPTER TWELVE

WHITE-HOT RAGE THAT anyone could be so cruel to her crystallized all the chaos of Alex's emotions as he held Maggie in his arms. He rocked her back and forth, stroked her hair, held her to him as if each of their lives depended upon it. Maybe not actual life and death. But he knew they were being given a chance here. A chance to set the world to rights. *Her* world to rights.

He wanted her, something fierce. And tonight he was going to show her exactly how beautiful she was.

As her tears eased, he held her out at arm's length then swept a few errant tears away from her cheeks. She was so beautiful. Exquisite, even. And every cell in his body ached to be with her.

"I think you're the most beautiful woman I've ever seen," he said.

It hadn't been what he'd planned to say, but it was true. He couldn't yet put a name to what he was feeling for her, but she could be sure it included respect and desire.

"You don't have to say that." She tried to wriggle free of his hands but he held her, determined to make her see that he meant it.

"I know I don't. And you don't have to say anything in return. But we both know there's been something between us ever since we met."

"Something we've both been pretty actively fighting," she pointed out. "There's got to be a reason for it."

She was being cautious. Now that he knew her full story, her fears, he understood her reluctance to follow through on the obvious sexual tension that had being zinging between them since that first day on the ferry.

"You're right. Absolutely right. We each had hurdles to cross. I definitely did. I needed to understand that what happened with Amy didn't happen to me...it just happened. She had milliseconds to make a choice. I probably would have done the same thing. Tried to help the patients. She was in an impossible situation." He reached to the top button of his shirt and undid it. "I guess now's as good a time as any to learn to let loose a little. Life is full of risks. Especially when there's a Maggie Green living right here under my roof."

Her soft smile warmed him through and through. "You don't mean that." She didn't sound convinced, so he plunged in at the deep end.

"Absolutely, I do. From the moment I met you, you turned my world upside down. Did I want to resist? Hell, yes. My son is my priority. And you know more than most I adhere to a rigid code of conduct, but when I see Jake with you? Playing games or cooking? Whatever it is the two of you do..." He shook his head as he pictured their heads tipped toward each other, laughing over some silly joke. "It makes my world light up. You make my world light up."

Light flared brightly in her eyes. It was time. The energy coursing between the pair of them was a powerful mixture of understanding, love and desire. It was sexy as hell.

He tipped her chin up toward him and kissed her. Softly at first. And then when he felt the tension in her body give a little, he pressed his hand to the small of her back and pulled her even closer. He wanted to taste and explore that beautiful mouth of hers. Catch that full lower lip of hers between his teeth then give it a slow, warm, swoop with his tongue. Soon any control he possessed had morphed into pure, raw need.

She flicked his switches. All of them. Hot and cold. Wary and elated. Grateful. Furious. And a thousand more he couldn't think of names for because all his body wanted right now was to be touching her.

In one swift move he shifted his feet to the floor then scooped her up in his arms.

"What are you doing?"

"Something I should've done the first day you came here."

Seconds later they were in the shower, fully clothed, her legs cinched round his waist as if she'd done it a thousand times before, each of them tipping their heads up, laughing as the steamy warm water poured down on the pair of them.

He knelt down so that he could put Maggie onto the chair that she used in the shower. He'd never felt such a powerful connection with a woman before. Two hearts, bare to the other. Two bodies he already knew were made for one another.

"Maggie Green..." Alex barely recognized his own voice it was so hoarse. "Would you do me the honor of allowing me to make love to you?"

For the first time ever Maggie felt shy in front of him.

"I wish I had on something a bit more...sexy." They both looked down at her saturated flannel shorts and plain cotton tank top.

"You don't need lingerie to make yourself look beautiful." Alex dipped in close and began kissing her neck just below her ear, his fingers running the length of her décolletage. Her breasts instantly responded to the light brush of his hand, the tingling sensations soaring in an arrow straight to that magic spot below her belly.

Oh, boy. She was in serious trouble.

She grabbed his face between her hands and forced him

to look at her, water pouring down both of their faces. She prayed he couldn't tell some of the droplets on her face were tears of disbelief.

"Are you absolutely sure this is what you want?"

"I'm absolutely sure you are *who* I want," he said.

And just like that, any fears she'd still had slipped away, leaving yet more room in her heart for Alex.

"Hang on a minute." He drew a finger along her jawline then dipped in for a deep, hungry kiss before jogging out of the bathroom.

He returned with a chair.

"To put us on an even keel."

She beamed. The man thought of everything.

He placed the kitchen chair he'd been using in his office opposite hers. Hers still had the wheels on it. He reached between her legs and pulled her to him so that his legs flanked hers. It was brusque and urgent. Mr. Protocol wasn't anywhere in sight. He was a hot, red-blooded male and when she saw the desire burning in his eyes, for the first time in her life she felt truly beautiful.

All his attention was focused on her as if the rest of the world had ceased to exist. He noticed which of his touches elicited a soft sigh, a wriggle of approbation, a low moan for more.

Her entire body felt alight with the need to be closer. To touch him. To put her hands on his bare skin.

She put her hand on his chest and said, "My turn."

She took her time unbuttoning his shirt, shifting her hands along his chest…smooth and muscled with just a scattering of hair around each of his nipples. Nipples she couldn't resist dipping toward and giving a saucy lick and swirl with her tongue. When she felt the vibration of his moan shift down his torso as she trailed her fingers along the center of his six-pack, she smiled. So this was what it felt like to love someone on an even playing field. You gave. You took. You shared. You pleasured.

A potent flash of sensuality snapped through her like a whiplash. "Stand up," she commanded playfully.

A little to her astonishment, he did. His trousers were plastered to his legs and right there in front of her was the taut, pronounced proof of his longing for her. He gasped when she reached out and pressed her hands against it, then leant forward, pressing her lips to the fabric as she undid the top button of his trousers then slowly worked her way down the full length of his fly until in one sharp move she yanked all the fabric in between her and his potency down his muscular legs.

"Step out of them," she said, her eyes glued to his erection.

He did.

She reached out and curled her finger along the top of his erection, enjoying the silky wet sensation of his response to her touch followed by another throaty moan.

"What are you doing to me, woman?"

She flashed him a naughty grin. "I'm hoping you'll give me the pleasure of making love to you."

She slipped first her hand, then her mouth down the length of him and lost herself in giving him the same amount of pleasure he had given her.

"Please…" He eventually pulled back when she could tell he was approaching a climax. "I want to wait. I want to be inside you."

He crouched down, cupped her face in his hands and kissed her as if it were their first and last moment on earth. By the time they'd finished it felt as if the world was somewhere brand spanking new and it had been created just for the two of them. A place to share and love. Heal. Nurture. Grow.

But right at this exact moment? What she wanted more than anything was to see exactly how long she could bear to keep fighting the urge to wrap herself around Alex's waist again and be lowered onto the solid length of his erection to bring that ever-deepening ache between her legs and his to a mutually satisfying release.

A grin crept onto her lips as she felt the water turn a bit cooler.

"What do you think about moving this party to somewhere a little more...dry?"

He looked down at her, laughed, turned off the taps and grabbed a couple of huge white bath towels sitting on a bench just outside the shower. Not only had they drained the hot-water tank, they were both in danger of getting prune skin. She looked at him, his green eyes twinkling, his body all strong and solid and beautiful. Yeah. He'd even look good with prune skin. It was then and there she knew she definitely wanted to grow old with him. The revelation, instead of blindsiding her, emboldened her.

A man she could not only admire professionally but laugh with in the midst of one of the most intensely sexual moments of her life?

"Come here, you." He pulled her to him again, gently this time, and wrapped her in a thick towel. He rose and tucked one round his waist, beads of water still wending their way along his chest. He lifted her up and carried her to his room and laid her on the bed, looking at her as if she were the most precious thing he'd ever come across.

By the time Alex had carried her into his bedroom, remembered he didn't have any protection, thrown her a medical journal to keep her company while he hot-tailed it over to the clinic to get some condoms, and come back again she had a full-on case of the giggles.

She nestled beneath the dark navy duvet as he shrugged off his long winter coat to reveal first his bathrobe and then, after she gave a sotto voce wolf whistle, he sexy danced it off to reveal his towel and then that scrumptious male body of his. This was a side of Alex she could get used to seeing much more of.

She almost wished she still had her prostheses on so she could sexy dance them off as well. Almost. Because knowing Alex desired her with or without them was more than enough to fill her heart to bursting.

She made a silent promise to herself to try not get too attached to him, but when he pounced on her and started tickling and kissing her, she felt like a naughty teenager and a screen siren all wrapped into one. More than that, she felt loved. Desired. The whole nine yards.

He switched the light off and stretched out alongside her, taking his lazy time as he brushed his fingers lightly over her breasts, her belly and then dipped into the sweet, hot, curves between her legs as he simultaneously lowered his tongue onto her taut nipple and lightly grazed it with his teeth.

"You are a saucy devil," she whispered as her body hummed and arched at each and every touch. He was good at this. Ridiculously good.

"As long as you're happy."

She could barely form words she was so happy. When he slipped first one finger and then two into the soft folds between her legs she could barely control herself.

"My turn."

With athletic grace she'd never felt before, she rolled over and straddled him, knees cinched at his hips, shifting herself against the solid length of his desire. The look in his eyes turned feral and when she put her hands down to touch the rigid heat of him, she felt pearls of his desire rise to the surface. She snapped her fingers. "Now."

Miraculously he knew what she meant and reached across and grabbed a condom, ripped it open and placed it atop his erection. She helped him slip it down the length of him and when she'd moved his hands to her hips, she slowly, teasingly, lowered herself onto him.

They both groaned with the ache of pent-up desire as he filled her. This was what it meant to make love. This was what passion should be about. Fast and slow. Deep and rich. Heightened awareness allowing them to tap into the ever-changing rhythms of their desire until, at long last, they lost themselves to passion and an explosion of plea-sure brought them together in a way neither of them had ever imagined possible.

Later, when she'd unpeeled her ability to speak from the ceiling and returned it to her body, she nuzzled in even closer to Alex and stretched an arm across his chest. "That was amazing."

"No." He felt him shake his head against the pillow then kiss the top of her head as he absently played with her hair. "That was out of this world."

Then, as if they'd done it a thousand times before, they both drifted off to sleep.

CHAPTER THIRTEEN

ALEX REGRETTED LEAVING Maggie on her own to wake up. What had he been thinking, putting her back in her room while she'd slept? Had it really bothered him that Jake might find them together?

He stared at his hands as if they would give him the answer.

Nope. Nothing there.

He leant back in his chair, praying for some sort of explanation to come to him. A reason why he had fled his own home before the sun had come up.

The truth hit him fast and furious.

He loved her.

He loved her and it scared the living daylights out of him. It scared him because loving Maggie meant, for the first time in six years, he would be looking forward, not back. Hoping, not dwelling. Living an entirely different life than the one he'd planned so carefully when he'd built this clinic.

He pressed his fingers into his temples, willing himself to get back up and go to the house and tell her. Tell her that he loved her. That he might not be a hundred percent into the handstands on horseback thing, but that the only way he wanted to go through life was with her on one side and Jake on the other.

He pressed his feet to the floor and tried to get up.

No good.

There was something missing from the equation. Something he had yet to identify.

He had love. He had the perfect woman.

What he needed now...was permission. And he knew exactly who he should be talking to.

Maggie entered the main door of the clinic with a dramatic little twirl as she pushed the door shut against the wind and light snowfall.

Happy, happy, happy.

When she'd woken up she had been in her own room, probably so Jake didn't find her in his daddy's bed. Alex must've carried her in there during her REM phase because she didn't remember a thing. He'd placed a chair by her bed with her "work" prosthetics on it, the ones with the gym shoes she favored, along with a fresh pile of clothes still warm from the dryer. Perfect. Just like him.

"Close that door! You'll let Jack Frost in and I'm not built for cold."

Maggie pushed the door shut behind her and beamed at Marlee. Wasn't Marlee great?

"It's seriously wintry out there." She and Marlee stared out the window at the deepening snow. Thank goodness the clinic's ground crew kept the paths clear. She'd have to remember to keep some crutches or a walking stick to hand just in case they grew slick with ice. Then again...*sigh*... she could always get a piggy-back from her new boyfriend.

Was he her *boyfriend*? Her heart did a whirly pop followed by a high-speed can-can. Her brain went on a little sing-song. She had a boyfriend.

Or maybe...her stomach lurched...

This wasn't history repeating itself, was it?

He left you breakfast. Jerks who leave a girl to stew in her own insecurities don't provide her with breakfast.

"Don't look so horrified, honey. It's snow! It don't bite."

Marlee grinned at her and Maggie did her best to return a smile without also spilling her guts. "We don't like to do things by halves here on Maple Island, do we, Doc?"

Maggie followed Marlee's gaze and saw Alex heading straight toward her. A fluttering of butterfly wings brushed against all the spots she wished they wouldn't.

"Good morning, Miss Green," Alex said in that slightly strangled Robot Man voice of his. "I was just—"

What? You were just what?

Her stomach lurched again. He looked a lot like he was pretending he hadn't slept with her last night.

"Morning! I was just…" She flicked her thumb in a random direction, trying to cover the fact she had actually been looking for him. Wanted to thank him for the breakfast he'd set out for her.

Everything about him pinged out at her in vivid detail… The clarity of his green eyes. The fact there was a little smattering of freckles just where he buttoned his shirt up… Her eyes dropped….it was buttoned up to the top again. That simple gesture sent her into a tailspin. Did this mean he didn't feel the same way about her as she did about him? As lovely as it had been—as *extraordinary* as it had been—there was no way she could stay on the island if Alex didn't love her, too.

What did she want? For him to unbutton his shirt down to his belly button?

A surge of frustration caught in her throat. She had turned a corner. She was ready. Ready to love someone again. Ready to love Alex. And here she was, standing in the clinic foyer of the man she loved, praying he felt the same way.

"Maggie?" Marlee and Alex were both staring at her now.

"Yes! Right. I'm just going to go get my wetsuit." She gestured toward Alex's house, although she knew perfectly well she'd left it hanging in the pool's changing room. Her heart wasn't the only thing that was short-circuiting. Her brain was just one big fog of white noise drowning out every single beautiful moment of the night she'd thought would be the start of her new eternity.

"Wait a minute." Marlee looked between the pair of them. "You're still staying with Alex?" If Marlee had been a dog, her ears would've been standing right up and her tail would've been going at high speed. Marlee, Maggie had learnt early on, loved a bit of gossip.

"Whoa!" she heard herself whinny as a flush crept up her neck. "Dr. Kirkland here was a little concerned about me staying up in the barn apartment without there being any other means of escape than the stairs."

"But that thing's been set up with an elevator for over a week now." Marlee turned to Alex with an expression of utter bewilderment.

What?

"Surprise," Alex said weakly, his fingers doing a very, very bad version of jazz hands.

She could've moved out over a week ago and he hadn't said anything? She'd have sworn he wasn't the type of man to keep things from her.

So maybe that meant he *did* love her. Or perhaps she was hoping he did when he actually had another reason for not telling her about it.

This time it was Alex's turn to color. Not in an obvious way. But if shifting his feet back and forth and refusing to make eye contact was his version of blushing, he was doing it in spades.

"There were still a few things I wanted the boys down at the volunteer fire station to check."

Was it a cover or was he asking her to move out?

Didn't he know how she felt about him?

Course not. You haven't told him.

Argh! She did handstands on moving horses, for heaven's sake, and she couldn't tell the man he'd won her heart pretty much the first time she'd laid eyes on him?

Marlee persisted. "I can get the boys down here this morning if you'd said." She reached for the phone and as one Alex and Maggie said, "No!"

They turned to one another, appalled.

Marlee began to busy herself with some invisible dust on the countertop.

The front door pushed open and Dr. Rafael Valdez walked in, brushing snow off his shoulders. "Beautiful day, isn't it?" He looked fresh and alert, ready to start by hitting the ground running on his first day at the clinic.

Alex grunted something indecipherable and nodded.

Marlee started wittering on about coffee and would Rafael like to have one. She knew they liked it dark and hot in Spain, so she could make a pot special. "Can I get either of you two anything?"

Maggie shook her head. She wouldn't need caffeine today. Or for the next month of Sundays. She'd be running on adrenaline from here on out because she needed to get a new job, a new home, and a new life as fast as humanly possible.

Or you could tell Alex you love him and see if he feels the same way about you. Like a grown-up.

Marlee took the moment's awkward silence to usher Dr. Valdez to the staffroom.

Fleur Miller clinked into Reception, still using her crutches, despite the fact Maggie knew Alex had been encouraging her not to use them.

"Maggie." Alex took a step toward Fleur. "You remember Miss Miller from our rounds, don't you?"

"Yes. I remember lots of things."

Like whether or not her boyfriend/not boyfriend had told her there had been an empty apartment sitting there waiting for her to move in to *over a week ago.*

She softened. There was also the fact that, only a few

hours ago, they'd held one another so closely she could feel his heartbeat.

She rattled off the details of Fleur's dancing injury and the rehab program she had been on.

Alex looked genuinely perplexed at her curt tone.

"Maggie, is everything all right?"

"Course. Why wouldn't it be?"

Then she circled back to the far more relevant question. Why hadn't he asked her to move out of his house days ago?

Because he just might feel the same way you do, nitwit. He surely wasn't just trying to get you into bed...

All of this—the insecurity, the panic, the weirdness—this was all her. The man had made her *breakfast*, for crying out loud. With chia seeds. He hated chia seeds.

He wasn't a bells and whistles kind of guy. What had she expected? A full-blown parade celebrating the fact she'd finally made love with someone who seemed to genuinely care for her?

Everyone was staring at her.

Too many thoughts. Too much to think about. She scrunched her eyes tight and gave them a rub. She was going to have to figure out a way to act normally. Not jump on the man and insist he spend the rest of his life with her right in front of everyone. He'd be mortified. She wanted him to love her, not panic about his life being a three-ring circus every five seconds.

She fixed her attention on Fleur.

"How long have you been using those?" Maggie knew she still sounded grumpy. Knew she lacked her usual charm. Tough. She was trying to dig herself out of an emotional avalanche and could really do with some alone time but, oh, well. They were here now.

Fleur glared at her and tightened her grip on the crutches. "I need them."

Maggie thumbed through the notes on her tablet. "No,

you don't. Not if you've been here since before Christmas. You should at least have graduated to a cane—or nothing by now."

Marlee was staring at her as if she'd turned into the Abominable Snow Girl. Well, maybe she had. She didn't have to be cheery and delightful *every* day of the week, did she?

Fleur crooked her head and gave Maggie a peculiar look. "Aren't we meant to be meeting in the pool?"

, "Yup. Absolutely." She turned brisk and efficient. And pasted on a smile. "Let's go down together. What do you think about not using the crutches to get there?"

Fleur gave her a quick *You are definitely the new girl* scan.

"If you want to find a wheelchair and take me to the pool that way, that's fine by me."

It obviously wasn't what Maggie had meant and Fleur knew it. She expected Alex to jump in and say something. He said nothing.

Maggie maintained her eye contact with Fleur. They were obviously both in dig-your-heels-in moods.

Terrific. Just what she needed.

One boyfriend with secret apartments lying in wait and a patient who had made it more than clear to all the staff that the last place on earth she wanted to be was right here on Maple Island. Her hometown.

Maggie tilted her head and gave Fleur a sidelong look. Something told her a dancer—a person who put themselves through so much physical pain—wasn't a quitter, so she tried again.

"You can use my arm if you give me one of the crutches."

Fleur gave her one of those looks intimating she was through answering ridiculous questions.

Maggie shrugged and put out her hand to guide the way, not even bothering to look at Alex as they passed him. See? She could do normal.

Oh, good grief.

As if she knew what normal was.

"What's up with you?" Cody was looking at Alex as if he had dyed his hair purple and started wearing sparkly jumpsuits to work.

Cody was a good friend as well as a colleague so he gave his answer some consideration.

He could answer honestly. He could say, "Everything. I think I just drove away the woman I love. My son will probably never speak to me again when he hears."

Or he could lie. Do what he and Cody always did and say, "Nothing much. Just a bit snowed under."

What he really wanted to do was drop his head onto his desk and hope the resulting bump made what had just happened in Reception a very, very bad dream.

Why had he been such an *idiot*? Maggie had obviously thought the worst about him keeping it a secret that the apartment was ready. She'd stormed off looking as miserable as Fleur usually did. Correction. *Always* did. The woman responded to staying at the clinic the way most people took to being sentenced to life in a high-security prison. He definitely wasn't going to ask her to post an online review of the clinic anytime soon.

He shook his head. *Oh, Maggie.*

Why had he just stood there like a lump? All he'd had to do was say he wanted her to stay. It was the truth. That's why he hadn't told her the apartment was ready. Every day he'd tried to make himself tell her and then he'd walk in on Jake and her caught up in some joke, or she'd catch his eye and they'd have one of those electrically satisfying smiles. The kind that made him think love could live in his heart again. And after last night? He knew exactly what he wanted to do. Propose. Tell her he loved her. Because, yes, that's what this was all about. Loving her. Embracing her. Embracing their future together and marrying her. Then they could spend the rest of their lives living life to the full and bickering about whether or not he should've told her about the apartment being ready.

He'd been up half the night planning the perfect proposal. The beach was the ideal location. Even in a snowstorm it was magical. He'd woken up Jake before he'd left this morning and asked him if he'd be the ring bearer. He could kick himself now for letting Jake in on the secret before he'd found out if Maggie was interested.

Idiot.

He'd even thought of throwing in a puppy. Jake's idea. Anything she wanted. Just so long as she said yes. Yes, she'd be his wife. Yes, she'd love Jake as if he were her own. Yes, she wanted to make a family with him. Be together forever.

Cody tapped his pen on the desk. He was waiting. Unusual. Cody usually had the attention span of a gnat unless he was with a patient.

"Nothing." Alex shrugged as if the question was an odd one. "Nothing at all."

"Yes, there is. There's been something funny about you recently."

Alex looked round him as if whatever it was Cody was noticing would pop up from behind his shoulder. A giraffe maybe? A goat?

Cody leant back in his chair in the office they sometimes shared and stared at him good and hard.

"It's not just the whistling."

"What whistling?"

"Oh, come off it, Kirkland. You know you've been whistling round the place like you're getting ready for some sort of audition." He squinted at him hard. After a couple of awkward rounds of the second hand in which Alex had plenty of time to wonder if this was what Cody's patients felt like, his business partner said, "I've got it. I know what it is."

"What? What *what* is?"

"What's weird about you. You were *happy* this morning. Now you're not."

He watched Cody watching him and felt powerless to do anything beyond give a *There you go, then* shrug.

A real powerhouse of communication, the pair of them. They'd always had one of those silent agreements that they simply didn't *go there*. The main thing they shared was a need to get things right for their kids. Make sure the children never had to go through the chaos of loss again.

That's when it hit him. He was the only one standing in the way of losing Maggie.

He needed to ask her to marry him. Here. Now. Without the plan. Without the ocean. Or the puppy. Even the ring.

"I think I'm in love," he blurted out.

If Cody was surprised by this admission he didn't look it. The man would be hell to play poker with.

"And I'm going to ask Maggie Green to marry me."

Cody arched a brow. "When you know, you know," he said.

Alex nodded as if they were simply passing old-timer wisdom back and forth. "Ain't that the truth."

"Well..." Cody lifted up a pile of papers he'd printed out, detailing some new research he'd found on the internet, and clonked them into place on the desktop. When he finished he turned in his wheelie chair and faced Alex. "What're you waiting for? Why don't you go and ask her?"

"Good question."

He sat there for a moment longer, staring at Cody but not really seeing him.

Yes, it was fast. Yes, it was intense. But it had been similar with Amy. Fast and furious. He'd met her on day one of boot camp and three days later he knew he wanted to spend the rest of his life with her. Turned out it had been the rest of *her* life and nothing more. But they'd *had* it. And what they'd shared had been that beautiful miracle of love. Now he was lucky enough to experience the miracle a second time. A *different* miracle. One that made him feel courageous and a bit freaked and proud and excited—excited for the future he would share with Maggie if she said yes.

Amy would've been the first one to be up in arms over his resolute bachelorhood. She'd always said to him each time either one of them had gone on tour, "I will always love you, but know that if I am ever taken away, you and Jake should *always* be loved."

And they were.

Maggie hadn't spelled it out, but he knew it in his heart. Had seen it in her eyes. And if he didn't get his act together, he was going to risk destroying the most beautiful thing he'd ever been a part of.

"Aren't you going to help me get out?" Fleur was staring at Maggie with utter disbelief.

"Nope." From the work they'd done in the pool, Maggie could see Fleur was more than capable of getting out of the pool on her own. Her crutches were just beyond the safety guard. She would stake her career on Fleur's ability to reach them unharmed.

If she could be bothered.

"This is the only time we're going to be working together, so I figure this is your one chance to show me what you got."

"What? I thought you were going to be my physio from now on."

"Nope. There's a new physio coming in. You'll love him."

"Why? Because he'll see sense and give me my crutches?"

"Nope again." Maggie didn't actually have a clue what the new physio would do. "He's British. Hearing things you don't want to hear always goes down better with an accent."

Fleur glared at her.

Maggie lay back and floated, willing herself not to think

of Alex's soft southern accent. She stared at the ceiling, completely unsurprised to see the bespoke finishing Alex had in place all around the clinic put there, too. At a glance it looked like a standard wooden beamed affair. Maple. Of course. But now that she looked at it more closely, smiling to herself a little as she heard Fleur begin to awkwardly wade to the side of the pool, she realized all of the cross-beams were recovered driftwood.

Oh, Alex. Her heart softened then squeezed so tight she began to sink. Maybe she really had misread things this morning. What had she expected? That he'd throw himself at her feet and declare his undying love for her? The staff were used to Dr. Protocol. Maybe he thought they'd all be weirded out by the funny, passionate, spontaneous man she knew existed behind that stuffed-shirt exterior of his.

The door to the pool room burst open and Alex stood framed in the doorway like a modern-day Clark Kent. Glasses askew. Khakis perfectly creased. An invisible cape just itching to break free from his light blue oxford shirt.

Damn, she wished his outside didn't make her insides go all gooey. How was she supposed to stay furious and angry with all that sexiness wrapped up in one big nerdy man package?

"Marry me," he announced.

Her legs stopped working and she went under before she got a grip and came up again, choking on the chlorinated water.

Fleur's attention had been grabbed. That, or she was hoping that when Alex had finished proposing he might hand her her crutches.

"Marry me," he said again. Insistently this time.

"But—"

"I messed up." He crossed to her, his sandy blond hair Einstein crazy, all of his energy focused on her. He was completely oblivious to Fleur, who was now leaning out of the pool and stretching toward her crutches.

Maggie started when water hit her face.

"What the—?"

Alex had jumped in the pool. Clothes. Shoes. Tie. The whole caboodle.

They really needed to stop having these baptismal-style rendezvous. They always led to kissing. And she wasn't up for kissing a man who wasn't prepared to acknowledge her in public.

"Marry me," he said when he surfaced. And he kept repeating it as he waded through the waist-deep water to get to her. "Marry me. Trust me. Have faith in me. Believe in me. Believe in *us*."

She stared deep into his eyes, her expression utterly sober. "You know there's a sign that says no jumping." She pointed to it.

"Sometimes you have to jump. Take a leap." His green eyes were blazing with intensity.

Right. He wanted to see this through? They were going to see it through.

"Why didn't you just tell me about the apartment in the barn?"

He shook his head. "Because I'm an idiot. Because I wanted you to stay—not because I was looking to scratch an itch, I swear to you. Because I couldn't find a way to tell you I loved you until now. And now that I know I do I'm trying to get my head wrapped round this new reality." He tipped his head to the side and gave her a sheepish grin. "That...and we'll probably have to move in there while the house is rejigged for you. I think we should put an elevator in there, too. Which means..." his expression grew playful "...you'll have to work on curbing that moan of yours with Jake in the room right next door to us. The walls up there are thinner than those in the house."

Against the odds—well, not really—she felt her heart soften further. Had she let herself fall back on old anxieties because they were more familiar territory? Was she brave enough to do everything he asked of her? Believe in him? Trust him? Believe they could be a family?

She heard the door slam as Fleur heaved herself out of the pool with her arms, snatched up her crutches and made her escape out of the hydrotherapy center.

She looked at Alex and shrugged. "I was hoping she might walk up the steps on her own, but perhaps the new guy will have more luck."

Alex stared at her as the water sloshed around them. "Marry me," he urged again in a whisper. "I love you."

"Even with these?" She pointed at her ultra-high-tech "water legs."

"Especially with those. I love *you*. Your heart. Your spirit. Your passion for life." He closed the space between them and cupped her face in his hands. "I love your lips. Especially when you're all emotional and they turn that beautiful deep red."

"They do—" She didn't finish. She couldn't. Alex's mouth descended on hers like those of a man seeking salvation, and who was she to deny a man passage from harm or loss? Especially when they kissed as well as he did.

When they each came up for air, forehead tipped to forehead, she whispered her greatest fear. "Will you ever be ashamed to be associated with me?"

He looked genuinely shocked. "Quite the opposite. I'll be the proudest man in New England! The world!" He picked her up and wrapped her legs around his hips. "I'll parade you around the entire clinic right now if you like. Just say yes."

"Don't you want to hear whether or not I love you?"

He brushed his fingers against her cheek. "How could you not?"

She laughed. "How very modest of you." She pulled back and gave him a solid look. "I love you, Alex Kirkland. And I love Jake, too. Not that you didn't already know that."

"So you're good about the fact that I come as a ready-made family?"

"Are you kidding? With you two as the starter kit? Does Jake know? Do you think he'll be all right with me being there as a mum? I mean, obviously I'm not a replacement mum, I—" Alex pressed a finger to her lips.

"Babbling?" she asked against his finger.

He nodded. "Jake will be ecstatic." Alex dropped a soft kiss onto her lips then murmured, "When do you think you might get around to saying yes?"

"I haven't said yes?" She was pretty sure she'd said yes.

"No, ma'am," he said in that low, slow, sexy drawl of his.

"Well, then... I guess I'd better."

She tipped back her head and sang it. As loud and as proud as she could.

"Yeeee-ssss!"

She hoped with every fiber in her body Marlee could hear her say it because then the whole rest of Maple Island would be in the know. She was a girl who said yes. Yes to life. Yes to family. Yes to being brave. Yes to taking risks, and most of all? Yes to being the girl who was going to marry Alex Kirkland.

CHAPTER FOURTEEN

"This is weird."

"What do you mean, it's weird? It's perfectly natural."

Maggie shot her husband a sidelong look and grinned. "You ever try carrying a bowling ball round in your belly and maintaining good balance?"

He reached out and rubbed her back. "We can always strap a real bowling ball onto my gut if you like."

"Ha! You don't have a gut. And what a good idea. Not." She laughed and turned to face him so she could slip her arms round his waist. "Oof. It's harder to reach your lips these days."

He leaned forward and gave her a soft kiss. "I think we could probably dream up some ways around that."

She dropped him a saucy wink. "I daresay you're probably right, but we've got to get to Jakey's hockey game."

"I can't believe you convinced me to sign him up for hockey."

"Don't you worry, Mr. Health and Safety. He'll be fine. I told the coach you'd be team doctor."

He huffed out a laugh. "I suppose we are going to be at every game."

"You bet. Jake's biggest fans!" She smiled and tipped her head onto Alex's shoulder. Jake actually had quite a few fans now. He'd really come out of his shell in the past year or so since the wedding and become, according to the teachers at his school, a proper leader. Jake had taken the opportunity to suggest that now would be a pretty good time to see if he was up to the challenge of having a puppy.

Which was why they were standing on the docks, waiting for the ferry and the "puppy fairy" to arrive.

"You sure you're up to this?" Alex swept a stray lock of hair away from Maggie's face.

"What? A baby and a puppy at the same time? Sure. I took you two on at the same time, didn't I?"

"What? I thought we were the ones who rescued you from a life of drifting around the world looking like a forlorn supermodel."

"Ha! I'll take the supermodel part. I was never forlorn."

"You were once."

She looked directly into her husband's eyes. "Yes. And I learned from it. Just like you learned from your grief. Maybe if we hadn't been through what we had, we never would've met." She took his hand in hers and gave it a quick kiss and a squeeze. "Meeting you changed everything—and if that means I had to go through a bad time to get there? It was worth every moment of it."

Alex dropped a kiss on his wife's forehead. "That's my silver linings girl."

"You betcha." She smiled at him, her heart so full she could hardly imagine fitting anymore love inside it. A little kick reminded her there was a whole lot more love coming soon. A baby girl, if the scan was right. Jake was already preparing to rescue her from any number of "princess perils."

"Right!" Alex gave her hand a swift rub as the ferry began to pull closer toward the docks. "You ready for a new phase of life to begin?"

"Always," she said. "With you by my side? I'm ready for anything."

* * * * *

LET'S TALK

Romance

For exclusive extracts, competitions
and special offers, find us online:

- facebook.com/millsandboon
- @millsandboonuk
- @millsandboon

Or get in touch on 0844 844 1351*

For all the latest titles coming soon,
visit millsandboon.co.uk/nextmonth